"You didn't answer me. Have we met before?" Randy asked.

Geoff merely smiled with a sensuous flicker of amusement that implied everything but revealed nothing. As he continued speaking on the phone, she saw red. Without thinking of the consequences, she grabbed the receiver from him and slammed it down. "I'm talking to you, and I want an answer!"

His emerald eyes caught fire as he turned to her. Gripping her by the arms, he whipped her around and backed her up against the wall in one swift, heart-stopping moment. Before she could catch her breath, he had her arms raised above her head and pinned to the wall.

"Are you crazy?" she gasped, straining against him.

"Certifiable," he said, "but at least I'm not rude. You didn't say please."

He kissed her before she could say please or anything else, kissed her with such shocking force and potency that all the air in her body seemed to get trapped in her lungs. She couldn't breathe for several seconds, and then she forgot all about needing to breathe, as the heat of his mouth enveloped her. . . .

WHAT ARE *LOVESWEPT* ROMANCES?

They are stories of true romance and touching emotion. We believe those two very important ingredients are constants in our highly sensual and very believable stories in the *LOVESWEPT* line. Our goal is to give you, the reader, stories of consistently high quality that may sometimes make you laugh, sometimes make you cry, but are always fresh and creative and contain many delightful surprises within their pages.

Most romance fans read an enormous number of books. Those they truly love, they keep. Others may be traded with friends and soon forgotten. We hope that each *LOVESWEPT* romance will be a treasure—a "keeper." We will always try to publish

LOVE STORIES YOU'LL NEVER FORGET
BY AUTHORS YOU'LL ALWAYS REMEMBER

The Editors

Suzanne Forster
Surrender, Baby

BANTAM BOOKS
NEW YORK · TORONTO · LONDON · SYDNEY · AUCKLAND

SURRENDER, BABY

A Bantam Book / March 1993

If you would be interested in receiving protective vinyl
covers for your Loveswept books, please write to this address
for information:

Loveswept
Bantam Books
P.O. Box 985
Hicksville, NY 11802

ISBN 0-553-44371-2

Published simultaneously in the United States and Canada

Bantam Books are published by Bantam Books, a division of
Bantam Doubleday Dell Publishing Group, Inc. Its trademark,
consisting of the words "Bantam Books" and the portrayal of
a rooster, is Registered in U.S. Patent and Trademark Office
and in other countries. Marca Registrada. Bantam Books, 666
Fifth Avenue, New York, New York 10103.

PRINTED IN THE UNITED STATES OF AMERICA

OPM   0 9 8 7 6 5 4 3 2 1

One

"*Pssssst*, Randy! This guy's the closest thing to an untamed animal I've seen outside the L.A. Zoo. Shall I send him in?"

Miranda Witherspoon glanced up from the work on her desk, wincing at the flushed excitement of her personal assistant, who'd just opened the office door a crack and stuck her head in.

"See if you can reschedule him, Barb," Randy pleaded, gingerly pressing her fingertips to a spot just above her right eyebrow and what promised to be the mother of all headaches. "The last applicant tried to bench press my file cabinet. And the one before that—with the shaved head and gargoyle tattoos—had hand grenades stashed in his camouflage fatigues. I saw them when he scratched himself. *Please*, Barb, make up some excuse."

"I'm not sure that's wise, Randy. He's not the type you pat on the bottom and point toward the door." Her voice dropped to a hush. "He looks like he could rip the buttons off your blouse with his teeth."

Randy shuddered. "Then tell him I've got PMS. Macho types are known to be terrified of mice and overwrought women. It's a male hormone thing."

Barb shot Randy a long-suffering look, mumbled something that sounded like "craven coward," and shut the door.

Randy continued to massage the tenderness above her eyebrow, one of the many trigger points for her tension headaches, according to her chiropractor. Her relief at postponing the appointment was mixed. She'd been interviewing mercenaries all morning, and if she'd known how difficult it was going to be hiring someone to find her missing fiancé, she would have tried an employment agency instead of taking out an ad in a soldier-of-fortune magazine. The men who'd responded so far looked more than capable of handling the job, but they'd all refused the assignment when she'd mentioned the Brazilian crime czar she believed was involved in her fiancé's disappearance.

Their reaction had magnified her fears about her fiancé's safety, and they'd also made her feel guilty for her suspicions about Hugh. She'd actually feared he might be getting cold feet about their upcoming wedding. It wouldn't be the first time she'd been left standing at the altar. But that fiasco was a long time ago, she reminded herself, part of her misbegotten youth.

As the pulsing in her forehead began to subside, she swiveled in her executive chair and gazed out the window of her tenth-floor corner office. The panoramic view of L.A.'s skyline was spectacular today, an imposing vista of mirrored skyscrapers etched against a cloudless blue sky. Sometimes she had to pinch herself to believe it was really true that she, Randy Witherspoon, a ragtag West Side kid, was head of market research for an international chain of resort hotels. Even more unbelievable, she was engaged to the firm's executive vice president in charge of acquisitions, Hugh Hargrove.

Edna would love this, Randy thought, sinking back into the chair's plush leather upholstery. With a wistful smile, she remembered her mother's dreams of a better life, of a Prince Charming who, complete with white charger, would sweep into their lives and rescue a beleaguered single mother and her young daughter from their bleak walk-up apartment. Even if Edna had gotten tangled up with some very questionable men while she was waiting for her prince to show up, she'd never stopped dreaming, right until the day she died five years ago.

A creaking sound alerted Randy that someone had opened her door. "Barb?" she asked, spinning around.

Randy's jaw dropped in utter surprise. It wasn't Barb who'd stormed the citadel. The job applicant filling Randy's doorway was at least six four. His storm-blown blond hair was as long, luxuriant, and wild as Randy's dark pageboy was neat, and the mirrored sunglasses hanging over the neckline of his T-shirt bounced the light from her windows like laser beams. If she'd had to describe him in ten words or less, she would have been tempted to call him a green-eyed golden mountain lion of a man.

"Did we have an appointment?" Randy asked.

"With destiny," he murmured.

Before Randy could think how to respond, he pulled a silver flask from his flak vest, walked to her desk, and handed it to her. "Might help with the PMS," he said, smiling with breathtaking sensuality. "It's a sure cure for hangovers."

"Uh . . . no thanks."

"I haven't got anything catching," he assured her. "And even if I did, this stuff would kill it."

Randy stared at the flask, wondering ironically if a shot of straight liquor might sober her up. Beyond her headache she felt a little drunk, probably from overexposure to testosterone. Impulsively, she took the flask from him and freed the cap. The brew that slid down her throat was unlike anything alcoholic she'd ever tasted. Tangy and sharp-edged, it stung as it went down.

"What is this?" she asked, clearing her throat.

He merely smiled, took the flask back, and helped himself to a deep pull before he returned it to his vest. The military fatigues he wore looked as if they'd seen action, especially the pants, which had prominent rips at the knee and thigh.

He was definitely a man who commanded attention, though not because he was classically handsome. The angles of his jaw were too blunt, and the bridge of his nose looked as if it had been broken more than once. And yet his green eyes, set like emerald chips in his sun-bronzed features, were undeniably striking.

"I'm answering your ad for a soldier of fortune," he informed her. He was oddly soft-spoken for such a big man, but the effect added to rather than subtracted from his physical presence. Burnished chest hair curled above the loose neckline of his T-shirt, and the biceps exposed by the rolled-up short sleeves were enormous. Even his hands were big. The right one had engulfed the flask he'd offered.

Brute strength, Randy acknowledged uneasily. If any words applied, those two did. Despite his quiet manner, he looked as if he could snap bones effortlessly. She glanced down at her own rather delicate arms, and beads of perspiration broke out on her upper lip. Whether it was the effect of the man or the drink, she didn't know, but she was beginning to sense that she was losing control of the situation.

How to End a Difficult Job Interview. Randy searched her memory, trying to recall that particular section of the book she'd read recently on guerrilla management tactics. *The interviewer should stand as a clear signal that the appointment has come to an end.*

She stood. "Actually, I'd finished interviewing for today," she said, favoring him with a courteous smile.

"So your assistant told me."

He made no attempt to leave; not even a muscle twitch indicated that he was getting the message. As she stared into his rich green eyes, Randy felt the strangest glimmer of recognition. It wasn't so much that she knew him from somewhere. She would have remembered him. It was more the sense that he knew her. There was a familiarity in his smile, and there was more than casual interest simmering in his eyes. Much more. It was almost . . . sexual.

What felt like a depth charge headed straight for Randy's stomach. *Why was he looking at her that way?*

"Why don't you sit down?" he suggested, whisking a straight-back chair from against the wall and setting it closer to her desk. "I'm going to."

The chair he'd chosen was several sizes too small for him, but he managed to look at home in it. Lounging down, he folded his arms casually, stretched out his long, long legs and gazed up at her with an air of expectancy that was unnerving.

Randy sat down too. Clearly the only way to regain control was to look as if she'd planned to interview him all along. "Do you have any experience locating Americans missing in foreign countries?" she asked.

"I've been working in recovery operations ever since I left the Marines, originally for the Pentagon, now on my own. Last year I brought back a U.S. diplomat who'd been detained in a Guatemalan prison camp and a missionary couple determined to save souls in the jungles of Brazil."

"Brazil? That's where my fiancé was last seen. He had business in Rio de Janeiro."

He hooked a foot on a rung of the chair and raked back a shock of white-gold hair out of his eyes. His smile was lazy, sexy, approving. "Rio, the city of sun, sin, and forbidden sex. Good place to get yourself lost."

"Hugh didn't get himself lost," she insisted. "He was last reported in the company of a man named Carlos Santeras, a Brazilian crime czar who's trying to go legit by buying into resort hotels. Santeras got his start in illegal arms dealing, jewel smuggling, and heaven knows what else."

She hesitated, waiting for the mercenary's reaction. This was where all the other he-men she'd interviewed had blanched and bowed out.

"Carlos Santeras?" He laughed as if remembering. "I haven't seen that pit viper since I rescued a female DEA agent from his jungle compound in the mountains several years back."

"You've dealt with him?" Randy asked.

"I doubt he'd put it that way. Let's just say I'm good at dodging machetes. I'm also intimately familiar with the converted subterranean slave quarters of his mansion where he kept the woman prisoner. . . ."

Randy listened with fascination as the mercenary went on, describing how he and his two former partners in recovery operations had gained entrance to the heavily guarded compound and then searched out the woman agent. As he recounted the story, Randy realized he was perfect for the assignment. He knew the area, and he'd already outmaneuvered Santeras once.

She waited for him to finish, intending to hire him on the spot, but as the seconds ticked by she became aware of some very strange sensations. She was beginning to feel flushed, as if the room's temperature had shot up ten degrees. Worse, her gaze seemed magnetically drawn to the more muscular parts of his body, and particularly to the way the material of his fatigues tugged at his spread legs. The man's thighs looked hard as marble. She could even see golden hair curling through one of the holes near his knee.

With some horror, she found herself following the path of his inseam, knowing exactly where it would take her. As her eyes crept upward toward the delta of his thighs, her heart began to pound frantically.

"Are you all right?"

Randy's head snapped up. "Yes, of course."

"Was it something I said?"

"No, I'd like to hire you, that's all. You're more than equipped—er, qualified to take on the assignment."

He was watching her with great interest, and she could feel her face heating under his scrutiny. He knew. He knew about her sexual fascination with his inseam. Avoiding his probing gaze, she lifted the collar of her blouse away from her damp skin.

"Are you interested?" she asked.

"Oh, yes . . . I'm interested."

She looked up. "In the assignment?"

"That too."

He continued to study her in a way that made her want to cross her legs and pull down her skirt. *What in the world was in that drink he'd given her?*

"What was your name?" she asked.

"Geoff Dias."

He said his name as though she ought to know it. Did she? She took a deep breath, gathering her wits. This was truly crazy. She had a crisis on her hands—her fiancé was missing—and she was fantasizing about a stranger. She never should have drunk from his flask. It had created an illusion of intimacy she couldn't shake. Had she already offered to hire him? Was it too late to change her mind?

"You're not dreaming," he said softly.

"What?"

Again that smile, lazy, sexy. It said everything and revealed nothing. He roused himself and sat forward on the chair, putting considerable stress on the rips in his fatigues.

"You said you wanted to hire me, didn't you?" he asked. "Maybe we should discuss the details?"

"Details, yes." Details were exactly what she needed right now—discreet bits of information, cool and concrete, reality-based. "My fiancé was supposed to have returned last week. When he didn't, I contacted his hotel, the airline, and, of course, the consulate. Everyone's been marvelously concerned and cooperative on the phone, but nothing's being done. Honestly, I'm at my wit's end. Hugh seems to have vanished, and all they want me to do is fill out forms." Her voice broke with frustration, emotion. "What if he's been hurt? We were to be married—"

"Married?"

"Yes, next month. The wedding's just two weeks away."

That bit of information seemed to take the edge off his sexy smile. He studied her left hand, where her engagement ring would have been if she hadn't been having it sized, then glanced past her, out the window, looking decidedly moody.

"Is everything all right?" she asked. "You are going to take on the assignment, aren't you?"

He rose, pulled a card from his vest pocket, and tossed it on her desk. "This is my fee, per day, plus expenses. I'll need some personal data on Hugh—a current picture, his driver's license, social security, and credit card numbers. I'd also like a thorough physical description and a list of his personal habits. You can fax it to me, the sooner the better."

"Fine," Randy said, startled by his abrupt behavior. She stood, too, concerned that he would leave before she was finished. "I'll see that you get the information. However, there is a condition to this deal we haven't discussed yet."

"Which is?"

"Me. I'm coming along, Mr. Dias. I'm going to Rio with you."

He barely reacted, except to give her a quick, insolent once-over as if she were a lame packhorse someone was trying to pawn off on him. "Sorry, I work alone. This is a dangerous assignment, *Ms.* Witherspoon. It's not Club Med."

Randy was more perplexed than offended. She hadn't expected him to be delighted, but she also hadn't anticipated being so rudely dismissed. "I won't get in your way," she explained patiently. "I'll stay in the hotel. I just want to be on the scene."

"You would be in the way, believe me. Especially if I had to get out of the country quickly."

She drew a breath and squared her shoulders. Politeness was getting her nowhere. "Mr. Dias, my fiancé is missing, and so far everyone I've appealed to for help has either patronized me, stalled me, or stonewalled me. They're not doing anything but shuffling papers, and I'm tired of sitting here feeling helpless! I'm *going*, and that's all there is to it."

"In that case you're going with someone else. I'm out." He nodded curtly and turned to leave.

"Mr. Dias!" she cried as he opened the door. "Don't be so hasty. We can discuss this, can't we? I'll pay you more than your normal rate—whatever you want."

He glanced over his shoulder and nailed her with a smoldering look. "You could never meet my price, Ms. Witherspoon," he said. "Trust me."

With that he shut the door and was gone, leaving Randy to stare after him in shock. "Well, *excuse* me," she murmured softly.

Taking one deep breath, she summoned the intestinal fortitude that had taken her all the way from the poverty of her childhood to this high-rise office. If any woman had ever pulled herself up by her bootstraps, Randy had. She'd worked two or three jobs, supporting her ailing mother and putting herself through college at the same time, all in the pursuit of a better life. Diligence had brought her this far. Diligence and a burning desire to succeed. It was the American way, her mother's dream, and to Randy's way of thinking, a West Side kid's only shot at success. Nothing had come easily, and because of that, she was used to putting her mind to something and then getting it, one way or another.

At the moment her mind was on Geoff Dias.

She walked out of her office and into the hallway just

in time to see him disappear through the exit door to the stairway. Of course, a soldier of fortune wouldn't take the elevator, she thought sardonically.

She caught up with him three floors from the bottom, no easy task in high heels and a short skirt. "I hope you don't think you can dismiss me so easily," she told him, fighting to catch her breath and keep pace with him at the same time.

He continued down the stairs at a good clip, apparently determined to do exactly that—dismiss her.

"Because that would be a mistake," she warned, speaking to the back of his massive shoulders and his streaming gold hair. Randy was a tad impatient by nature, and if she had little tolerance for being dismissed, she had even less for being ignored. Of all the arrogance! He wasn't even going to speak to her.

She reached out to touch him and jerked her hand back as he stopped on the landing. He glanced back and scorched her nearly senseless with a hot, proceed-at-your-own-risk stare. "'Easy' isn't the word that comes to mind in your case," he said.

"What word does come to mind?"

"Coward, maybe?" He started down the next flight.

"*Coward*? What's that supposed to mean?" Randy followed in hot pursuit, aware that it was the second time she'd been called a coward that day. First kiddingly by Barb, and now by him. Although Randy admitted to having her share of character flaws, she had never considered cowardice one of them. She'd always had to fend for herself, to fight for her dreams. She'd come a long way, but it had never been easy, and the risk of failure had always been great. "Are you going to explain yourself?" she asked.

"Probably not." He loped down the remaining flight, taking the steps two at a time, then shouldered open the exit door and rushed through.

Randy determinedly followed him, and let the door crash shut behind her. She found herself in an alley she barely knew existed, staring at a chrome monster of a motorcycle. Blinking in the bright sunlight, she tried to get her bearings. She still felt a little woozy and disoriented, probably from that drink he'd given her.

Geoff Dias swung a long leg over the gleaming black motorcycle and settled himself in the leather seat. With his long hair glinting gold, he looked like a Nordic god of warfare caught in the wrong time period. But the heated message in his gaze was anything but warlike. It said he could take her on the ride of her life if she was woman enough to climb on behind him.

Randy was certainly woman enough, but she had a long-standing aversion to motorcycles, and that included the men who rode them. As dearly as she'd loved her mother, Edna had harbored a weakness for just such men, beautiful losers and handsome rogues, men who caroused, couldn't hold a job, and often survived by living off lonely, susceptible women.

Every one of them had a get-rich-quick scheme, and Edna's romantic nature was so strong and her need to believe so great, she'd fallen for it every time. She'd died tragically young, in her late forties, of a congenital heart ailment, but Randy had always maintained it was love that killed her. She believed her mother had died of a broken heart.

"Did you follow me down here for the exercise?" Geoff asked. "Or did you have something in mind?"

Randy felt a bead of moisture trickle into the cleft between her breasts and realized her whole body felt warm and flushed. "Actually, there is something you can clear up for me."

"Such as?"

"Were you born arrogant, Mr. Dias? Or do you have to work at it?"

His slow smile could have dropped a charging rhino in its tracks, assuming the rhino was female.

"It's probably genetic," he admitted. "Like your temper."

"My temper? A moment ago I was a coward, and now I have a temper?" She hesitated as another vague glimmer of recognition took hold. There was something familiar about him—the way he held himself, his facial features—that plucked at a distant chord of memory. Why hadn't she noticed that before?

"And by the way, why *did* you call me a coward?" she asked. "You don't even know me."

He leaned forward on his bent knee. "Are you saying you aren't one?"

"What? A coward? Of course not."

"Care to prove it?"

The quickest way to prove her courage at that point would have been to decorate his big, strong jaw with a palm print. The thought alone gave her a stirring of satisfaction.

"You're smiling?" he said in that dangerously soft voice of his. "What's that all about?"

"Trust me, you don't want to know." Randy would have loved nothing better than to turn around and stroll out of Geoff Dias's life forever. There was just one thing preventing her. She needed him, dammit. He might be the only man who could find her missing fiancé.

"Couldn't we discuss this like two rational adults?" she asked, brushing dark hair from her face and straightening her navy blazer jacket.

"Discuss to your heart's content. I'm not going anywhere"—he glanced at his gunmetal-black pilot's watch—"for the next sixty seconds."

Lord, he was exasperating. She could feel her blood rushing with the urge to commit some sort of grade school terrorism, like kicking the fender of his bike. Worse, it annoyed her that he'd so easily found—and pushed—her panic button. With her professional success she'd come to pride herself on being coolheaded and pragmatic. She'd tried very hard to cultivate those traits and to leave behind all traces of her difficult childhood, including her impatience and her quick temper.

"All right," she said evenly, "let's discuss this. The problem is simple enough. I want to go, and you don't want me to. What if I agree to let you run the show? You can call the shots. The instant you think it's getting dangerous, I'll get on a plane and come home. How does that sound?"

"Crowded. I work alone."

"Mr. Dias, you're being unreasonable. I'm not asking to work with you. I just want to be there. I'm not the type who can sit home and wait. After all, it's my fiancé who's—"

"No deal," he said, cutting her off.

Randy felt the sharp sting of frustration. "Well, then, what *do* you want?" she asked. "What would it take to persuade you?" It was the wrong question, of course. She knew that the minute she asked it.

Dias settled back on the chopper, looking negligent and cocksure of himself as he made a leisurely pass over her dress-for-success outfit with his eyes, taking the deluxe tour this time. His gaze darkened, heating the strategic darts and seams, burning her flesh right through her clothing.

"Oh, yes, *that*," she said. "I suppose if I were to lift my skirt, show a little thigh, promise some action—"

"Now that you mention it," he agreed softly.

Randy glared at him. She couldn't believe he was serious! The silence between them stretched taut until it vibrated.

"You lied, Ms. Witherspoon," he said finally.

"I beg your pardon?"

"You said you weren't a coward." With that he twisted the ignition key, released the clutch, and gave the kick-start pedal a couple of quick pumps. Rising up, he stomped it hard, and the engine roared to life like a snarling, snorting beast. The message was clear. Geoff Dias was history.

Randy's heart began to pound. It hardly bothered her that motorcycles frightened the life out of her, or that he was about to ride off into the sunset, leaving her in the lurch. It was that one damn word that rang in her ears. Coward!

Spurred on by her own quickening pulse and the sexy challenge in his green eyes, she walked over to his rumbling bike, rested the toe of her spectator pump on the fender and drew up her slim navy skirt. Staring him straight in the eyes, she unhooked the lacy black garters hidden beneath her eminently sensible outfit.

It wasn't until she'd released the silky black nylon and was drawing it seductively down her thigh that it began to dawn on her what she was doing. Good Lord! A spur-of-the-moment striptease for a biker in a back alley? Her hands were trembling and she was damp all over. *What in the world was in that drink?*

Too proud to back down, she kicked off her shoe, whisked the damn nylon off, and tossed it at him.

Geoff caught it, laughing, and brought the sheer black silk to his face as if to inhale her female scent.

Randy's heart was pumping furiously as she stepped back from the bike. She felt as if she were coming out of some kind of hypnotic trance. Her behavior was wildly at odds with the conservative, professional image she'd worked so hard to achieve. "What have you done?" she asked him. "Drugged me? Is that why I followed you down here? Is that why I'm undressing in an alley?"

"Maybe you're undressing because you've got a fatal yen to get hot and sexy on the back of a great big bike."

"I beg your—"

"Sweetness, if you're begging for something, it's not my pardon." With that he tucked the nylon stocking in his vest pocket and revved the engine.

Trembling in places she'd forgotten she could tremble, Randy watched him roar down the alley on his bike and disappear from sight. The image of the gleaming motorcycle and his flying hair sent another frisson of

awareness through her. Where had she seen him before?

She glanced down at her stockingless, shoeless foot
and shook her head in disbelief. Not an hour ago she'd
been interviewing him in her office. How had she
managed to get herself in this condition? She could still
see his vibrant green eyes and the irresistible challenge
they harbored. She could see Geoff Dias as clearly as if
he were sitting on the bike in front of her, taunting her
with his lazy, let's-get-it-on grin.

Starting toward the scuffed pump she'd kicked off,
she felt a stirring of the competitive instincts that had
always seen her through do-or-die situations in the
past. By the time she had her shoe back on and her
skirt smoothed down, she was more determined than
ever to change his mind. It's not over until it's over, Mr.
Dias, she vowed silently.

Two

At twenty-eight Randy didn't think of herself as sheltered, especially having grown up in the streets of Los Angeles, but there were still a few things in life she hadn't experienced. One of them was the sacred male confines of a workout gym, complete with a boxing ring and sweaty bare-chested men wearing mouthpieces, gloves, and little else.

Not that she wanted to experience a men's gym. She wouldn't have been sitting in her car parked across the street from one right now if Geoff Dias hadn't been inside. In their interview the day before, she'd learned he ran an agency called Stealth International in downtown L.A. She'd pulled up across from his small office this morning, just in time to see him stroll out the door in faded gray sweats and then stroll into the gym next door. Her curiosity piqued, she'd been watching for another glimpse of him ever since. That had been a half hour ago.

"I suppose I'll have to go inside," she murmured, aware that women on the streets were fair game in this part of town. It wasn't too far from the neighborhood where she'd grown up, but things had deteriorated even further in the years since she'd been gone. She glanced down at the length of leg her wraparound dress revealed. Was a miniskirt safe under the circumstances? she wondered, letting herself out of the car.

She had the answer the moment she entered the sacred confines. She might as well have been dancing naked and clanging castanets, the way the boys whooped and whistled.

Reluctant to encourage them in any way, Randy hesitated a few feet inside the door and quickly scoped out the place, looking for someone safe to approach. She was hoping for a manager type, one of those grizzled old-timers who were supposed to hang out in seedy gyms according to late-night movies, but no such luck. The only two men in the place who weren't ogling her were in the boxing ring, trying to commit assault and battery with their bare feet.

Kickboxing, she realized, immediately intrigued by the fact that Geoff Dias was one of the boxers. She edged away from the rogue's gallery of leering males, hoping if she ignored their horseplay they'd realize she wasn't interested in "snapping their jockstraps," or any of the other equally lewd things they were suggesting.

A spot near the watercooler gave her a better view of the ringside action. Dias was good, she admitted, watching him spin and kick. Fast too. He struck with the velocity of a lightning bolt, his timing instinctive. There was a split-second hesitation, highly charged, followed by an electric arc of the body, a flash of limbs and sinew.

Randy wasn't surprised by his athletic ability, but he seemed too big a man for the agile grace required by the sport. Kickboxing was almost dancelike in its execution, and quite beautiful, she realized. But very swift, very lethal. As Geoff dodged his opponent's slicing jabs and returned them, his long blond hair flowed against the motion of his body, adding to the symmetry.

Though she tried to avoid fixating as she had the day before, she couldn't avoid the fact that he looked very nearly naked. The shorts and loose tank top he wore revealed the honed physique of someone who pumped iron, and yet he wasn't muscle-bound. Resilience shimmered in every movement. Even the muscles of his legs rippled fluidly, like water flowing over steel.

As the sparring match ended, Randy sensed a problem between the two men, though she couldn't hear what they were saying. Geoff turned away, and a shout of surprise went up as the other man attacked him from behind, landing a brain-rattling kick to the back of his skull. Geoff spun and lashed out with his foot, connecting with his opponent's jaw. The man staggered, shaking off the effects, but his lip was clearly bleeding. With a howl of anger he came at Geoff again.

Geoff dodged and whirled, a dizzying blur of motion as he flew through the air. He struck the man with a kick to the side of the head and sent him sprawling against the ropes. The hostilities seemed to be over until the other boxer recovered and sprang back, forcing Geoff to move in for the kill.

Shocked by the sudden violence, Randy looked away. A shudder passed through her as she registered the sounds and smells of physical aggression. Her nerves recoiled at the sickening impact of flesh on flesh. She'd always found blood sports appalling, and boxing was no exception. Yet now, having seen Geoff Dias in action, she was more convinced than ever that he was the man for her mission. He had an instinct for violence, for self-preservation. He could protect himself, and her too.

Now all she had to do was convince him to take the assignment. And get out of this gym in one piece, she reminded herself, aware that several of the men were still eyeing her as if she were the sparring partner they would most like to go a few rounds with.

"Are you looking for me?"

Randy turned to see Geoff climb through the ropes and drop to the floor. Blood oozed from a cut on his temple and sweat sheened his body as he walked toward her. He'd already pulled off his gloves, but he was still breathing heavily from the exertion, and she could almost see the heat rising off his brawny shoulders.

Randy's pulse raced out of control as he came to a stop just inches from her. He even smelled of the kill—of male power and animal instincts, of steamy sweat and last night's liquor. It was a pungent combination, still humming with the threat of physical force.

"Yes, I was looking for you," she said, refusing to give way to the trepidation that thinned her voice. "I was hoping we could talk."

"Talk?" He looked her over, lingering on the slit of her wraparound skirt as if considering the possibilities. "I was hoping for the rest of the striptease. Or at least a matched pair of nylons."

There it was, that lazy, sexy smile again.

He was baiting her once more, Randy realized. He might look deadly, but that flash of emerald in his eyes was nothing more than another sexy challenge. Damn if he didn't make her want to take her clothes off, just to show him!

"I only strip for total strangers," she informed him sweetly. "However, if it's nylons you need, there's a supermarket down the street. Try support hose, queen size."

A grin flashed—quick and cocky, irresistible. "On second thought," he said, wiping away the moisture that was trickling down his face, "what I need is a shower. You're welcome to come watch."

Her grimace let him know what she thought of that idea. "No thanks, sport. I'll just wait here."

"Not a good idea."

"What?"

"Waiting here. I'd advise against it."

"Why?"

He indicated the pack of gym rats who had greeted

her when she came in. "The natives are restless, and a tender little morsel like you would provide them with countless hours of entertainment pleasure. I've got a thought—"

"Oh, I'm sure you do, and good luck hanging onto it." She nodded curtly and turned toward the door. "Let me know when you're done with your shower. I'll be waiting in my car."

"Randy—"

She kept walking.

"*Ranndeee*—"

Sighing, she turned back to his roguish smile.

"Great ass," he assured her, his laughter shimmering with husky masculine nuances. "I was going to suggest that you park it on a chair in my office next door. You'll be safer there."

His office, roughly the size of a large walk-in closet, looked as if it had been decorated by teenage vandals. There was no receptionist in sight, no typewriter, no file cabinets, and no place to sit. Randy couldn't have parked her "great ass" if she'd wanted to. Even his desk chair was piled high with mercenary newspapers, gun catalogs, maps, telephone books, and the requisite girlie magazines.

His filing system consisted of stacked boxes full of folders. Fortunately, she wasn't hiring him to do clerical work. A busy mercenary probably didn't have time to file, she conceded, trying to be charitable as she surveyed the posters on his walls—of guns, of naked women, of naked women with guns. He wasn't shy about his personal preferences.

Randy felt less and less charitable the longer she waited for Geoff Dias, and by the time he strolled in, some forty-five minutes later, she was exasperated.

"What took you so long?" she asked.

He hooked a thumb in the ripped-out sleeve hole of his sweatshirt. "I wanted to look presentable."

Presentable, indeed. He was wearing the same sweats he'd had on when he entered the gym, but what she hadn't noticed then was the way they hung on his body, loose here, clinging there, especially to his lower torso. Nearly threadbare in places, the cotton material seemed to have formed a permanent attraction to certain parts of his muscular thighs and backside, accentuating every ripple and bulge.

For Randy, who preferred cerebral types like Hugh, Geoff Dias was one of the most blatantly physical men she'd ever encountered. And easily one of the most sexual, she admitted reluctantly. It was almost impossible to be in his presence without envisioning naked, flexing muscles and gleaming flesh. She even found herself imagining feverish sounds—virile grunts and moans, gasps of gratification. Weight lifting, she told herself. That's all the naked muscles were doing. Pumping iron!

"What can I do for you?" he asked amiably.

"You can quit playing games," she said, more irritated by the way her thoughts were straying than by anything he'd done. Every encounter with him was a tug-of-war, and she felt as if she were constantly losing ground.

"I don't have time for such nonsense, so let's get down to business, shall we?" She opened her purse, took out a stack of twenties and set it down on his desk. "This is twice your fee for one week's work. Are you going to take the job or not?"

He settled himself on the desk, then picked up the stack and thumbed through it, counting the bills. It was a lot of money, and Randy could only hope that a man of his seemingly modest means would be reluctant to pass up such a windfall.

"Twice my fee?" he said, glancing up. He set the money down, drew a twenty off the top and began to roll the bill into a tight cylinder. When he finished, he slipped the twenty between his fingers as if it were a cigarette he was about to bring to his lips. "That's a lot of cash," he said softly.

Randy resisted the urge to back up as he rose and walked toward her. She couldn't imagine what he intended, but she grew very still as he touched the rolled bill to her mouth lightly, then increased the pressure, denting the fullness of her lips. She wanted to turn away, but fascination kept her from doing it. Her senses were thrumming with anticipation. Her mouth had gone dry, her palms wet.

What was he going to do?

A whisper of cool air answered her question. With a soft jolt of alarm, she realized he'd slipped his index finger inside the neckline of her wraparound dress. He was lifting the silky material away from her skin. She glanced down as he exposed her breasts to his view, creamy half-moons swelling from the cups of her black lace demi-bra. Erotic glimpses of pink aureole were also visible. A pulse began to tick in her throat.

His breathing deepened as he studied what he'd exposed. His hesitation gave Randy a twinge of satisfaction. She had no idea what he'd expected to see, but apparently it wasn't black lace and partially exposed nipples.

Unfortunately, he regained his composure quickly.

Withdrawing his hand, he cupped her chin and brought her head up slowly, challenging her to meet his gaze. Weakness washed over Randy. His emerald green eyes were catlike, rich and hypnotic. Again, she had that flash of déjà vu, even more powerful than the day before. Why did she feel as if she knew him from somewhere?

"Have we met before?" she asked. The question evaporated in a rush of sensation as he began to stroke her cheek with his thumb. The pleasure of his touch was so intense, so unexpected, that Randy couldn't move. Her legs felt weighted, her ankles unsteady. She was aware of several things at once—the heat of his skin, its sensual pressure, and the edge of his thumbnail, gently abrading, sharply pleasurable. Deep in her stomach, muscles tautened.

She had no idea how long he held her spellbound that way, caressing her face while he touched her with the tightly rolled bill in more and more intimate ways. His fingers grazed her skin as he drew the money down her throat and over her collarbone, raising a flushed trail of excitement on her pale flesh. When his hand reached the trembling warmth of her cleavage, it stopped. He stared into her eyes, smiling.

"I thought I told you, sweetness," he said. "You can't afford me."

He tucked the bill deeply into her bra, brushing his knuckles up against her taut nipple, caressing her naked flesh and generally taking lewd and unfair advantage of her frozen astonishment to his heart's content before he released her. Randy's reaction was a choked protest. Before she could manage much else, he'd removed the offending hand and stepped back.

She watched in bewilderment as he walked to the desk, picked up the telephone, and jabbed a number as if she weren't there.

"What are you doing?" she asked.

"Making a phone call."

"Couldn't it *wait*? We're having a fight!"

"A fight about what?" He glanced at her over his shoulder. "You made me an offer. I turned you down."

"You fondled me!"

"Yeah, I did, didn't I?" His irreverent gaze came to rest on her breasts.

"Stop that! You perverted—"

He waved her silent. "*Buenos días*, Rico! *Cómo está usted?*" he shouted as whoever he'd been calling came on the line.

Randy felt as if she'd had a bucket of cold water

thrown in her face. She could hardly believe the arrogance. If she'd had any doubts about Geoff Dias's go-to-hell attitude, the back of his sweatshirt answered them when he turned full around. Printed in neat block letters were the words UP YOURS, AMIGO. Apparently, he'd read the book on guerrilla management tactics too.

She was too angry even to consider the intelligent solution, which would have been to cut her losses and leave. Her competitive instincts had been triggered yesterday by the first glint of his green eyes. By now they were armed and ready. She had no intention of giving up her quest to hire him, but her anger at the moment had more to do with salving wounded pride than with failed business negotiations. Outrage didn't seem to have the slightest affect on him, and as much as she might have wanted to snatch the phone out of his hand and carry out the instructions on his sweatshirt, she couldn't let herself. Cool heads prevailed, she reminded herself. She had to collect her wits and be as cool as he was. Cooler.

Her chiropractor had given her some breathing techniques for eliminating tension, but she needed something faster, something foolproof.

"E . . . N . . . O," she murmured, mentally reciting each letter as she said it out loud. "O . . . W . . . T." Counting to ten might work for others, but like a high-performance race car, Randy's temper required more sophisticated braking power. Years ago she'd started spelling the numbers backward as she counted. It required sufficient concentration that she often forgot what she was angry about before she got to ten.

She was on ytnewt-enin as Geoff hung up the phone.

"I'd like a moment of your time," she said politely.

"Try me tomorrow." He punched out another number.

"Perhaps you didn't hear me." But her protest fell on deaf ears. He was already immersed in another conversation.

"Y—T—R—I—H—T." Staring at his back, Randy pronounced each letter of the number slowly and through clenched teeth. Cool heads be damned, she thought, glancing up at the posters on his wall. If any of those guns had been real, Geoff Dias would have been a dead mercenary.

By the time he hung up, she'd abandoned counting techniques and regressed to thinking murderous thoughts. Only her voice was cool as she spoke. "What do I have to do to get your attention, Mr. Dias?"

"Are you still here?" he said, glancing her way.

"Am I still—" The last word jammed in her throat. Something about his profile stopped her. From that angle he looked suddenly, frighteningly familiar. Was it his jawline? The ridge in his broken nose?

"You never answered me," she said suddenly, urgently. "*Have we met before*?"

He merely smiled, that same infuriatingly sensual flicker of amusement that implied everything and revealed nothing.

As he turned back to the phone, Randy saw red. "Are you going to answer me, dammit?" Without giving a thought to the consequences, she walked over, snatched the phone receiver out of his hand, and slammed it into the cradle. "I'm talking to you, Mr. Dias. And I want an answer!"

His emerald eyes caught fire as he turned to her. Gripping her by the arms, he whipped her around and backed her up against the wall in one swift, heart-stopping movement. Before she could catch her breath, he had her arms raised above her head and pinned to the wall.

"Are you crazy?" she gasped, straining against him.

"Certifiable," he said. "But at least I'm not rude."

"*Rude*?"

"You didn't say please."

He kissed her before she could say please or anything else, kissed her with such shocking force and potency that all the air in her body seemed to get trapped in her lungs. She couldn't breathe for several seconds, and then she forgot all about needing to breathe. The heat of his mouth enveloped her, melting her unwilling lips, stroking and shaping them to his, mastering her responses. She knew that if he had his way, he would ultimately master the rest of her as well.

He was a big man, but it wasn't just his size that made her feel helpless. The instant his mouth touched hers, she was lost in the kiss. It was hot and heavy and punishing, an act of conquering, as if he was determined to prove something, to force her to acknowledge him. Why? she asked herself frantically. Who was he?

She tried to move, but he pressed her to the wall with his hips, forcing a soft moan out of her. He wanted something more than a stolen kiss, Randy realized with shocking clarity. Even more than the physical act of sex. *He was calling for unconditional surrender.* That awareness swirled through her senses as feverishly as hot steam.

Again she tried to move, and again he reacted swiftly, bringing her arms down, anchoring them alongside her head. He pressed his forearms to hers and held her fast, easily subduing her efforts to escape.

"Temper, temper," he said, his voice husky with passion. He grazed her mouth lightly with his, but instead of kissing her, he nipped the flesh of her lower lip.

Randy recoiled at the stinging pleasure. Why was he doing this to her? And why was she responding? She wanted to resist. She was trying to resist, damn him! And yet everything he did sent urgent thrills spiraling through her. The feel of his body flush up against hers melted her defenses, making her feel weak and heavy, weighing her down with sensations. The heat of his thighs seemed to flow into hers, and the power of his arms made her dizzy.

"Open your mouth," he murmured.

No, she thought. Never! She meant to tell him that, but as she parted her lips, he stole into the warmth of her, sweeping deeply into the vault of her mouth with his tongue. Randy's legs nearly buckled with the pleasure as he began to stroke into her rhythmically, his tongue repeatedly penetrating the soft barrier of her lips. If he hadn't been holding her, she would have sagged to the ground.

It was all so shockingly exciting.

It was all so terribly familiar!

"How does it feel, Randy?" he asked, whispering against her mouth, then breaking the kiss to search her face. "After all these years?"

She didn't answer him. She couldn't, not with her senses spinning wildly. He held her gaze with his eyes and pinned her to the wall with his lower body. He was aroused, hard enough to commit sin on a Sunday, and he wanted her to know it.

"Remember, baby?" he said softly, grinding his hips into hers.

Randy swallowed an anguished sound and slumped against the wall. Her stomach clutched as he pressed himself into its quivering softness. The motion of his hips was slow and grindingly sensual, as if he meant her to feel every twitch and throb of that one part of him. Lord, she did! He felt huge against her, and beautifully hard. He was forcing her to think about the act of lovemaking, about how all that rigid male flesh would feel inside her!

Remember, baby? Was that what he'd said? She couldn't remember anything but the steel heat and power of the man's body. She couldn't remember anything but the crazy pleasure of hard, deep lovemaking. The rocking of his hips had touched into some primitive female response and left her in a state of whimpering helplessness.

Remember, baby? *Surrender, baby* . . .

He picked her up and carried her to the desk, sweeping the papers and debris off it as he laid her down. He was going to make love to her right there on the desk, and Randy wasn't sure she had the power to stop him. Maybe she didn't want to stop him!

She waited for him to join her, but instead he stood beside the desk, his golden hair swirling forward, falling across his face as he looked down at her. He combed the hair back with his hand, revealing the unbridled sensuality in his features, the fever-brightness of his eyes.

He looked hot, hungry, ready to devour any woman who stepped in his path. The cords of his neck stood out, and the muscles of his biceps were thick with tension. He was too much man for her, she realized. Far too much.

A sound shook on her breath, sweet, sharp.

He reached down and slipped his hand inside the neckline of her dress, daring her to stop him as he caressed her breast. She couldn't stop him. She couldn't! Everything he did sent paralyzing currents of excitement through her. Her body reacted to the stimulation as if it were addicted, quivering with anticipation, trembling for more.

His green eyes bored into hers, forcing her to find the answer she'd been searching for. "Do you remember me now?" he asked, breathing hard. "Dupont Street, around midnight. The guy on the motorcycle."

Randy let out a soft shriek and scrambled off the table on the opposite side from him. "Oh, my God!" she said, staring at him, narrow-eyed. She began to back away as the realization hit her full force. "You couldn't be him! You *couldn't.*"

Three

"You're him?" Randy whispered, horrified. "The one on the bike?"

"How quickly they forget," Geoff said. "I'm hurt."

"But it *couldn't* have been you," she insisted, refusing to believe it even though her churning stomach told her it was true. "His hair was short—military short—and he was wearing those damn sunglasses. I never saw his eyes."

"You saw my eyes, Randy. You gazed real deep. You just don't remember. It was the middle of the night and you were flying high."

"I was not high. I was upset. I was crying."

"You were hotter than a smoking pistol."

"Stop it!" She turned away from him, shaken. She'd put out of her mind that ghastly night ten years ago the morning after it happened. But she had never come to grips with what she'd done that night, or forgiven herself for it.

Geoff Dias. He'd never even told her his name. Hearing it now gave her the chills because it made him real. It made what happened between them real . . . a forbidden encounter with a beautiful drifter on a motorcycle, a man with no name. That entire night had been wanton and surreal, the darkest kind of fantasy imaginable. Up to now it had been easy to pretend that it had all been a bad dream.

She swung back to face him, searching his features, still trying to convince herself it wasn't him. His hair was different, longer and biker-wild, a shotgun blast of white and gold, but his features held undeniable similarities. He was ten years older and his face was craggier, but he was still arrestingly attractive. If anything, he was more appealing. He was unquestionably more dangerous!

But how had he found her after all this time? "Why did you answer my ad for a soldier of fortune?" she asked him. "What do you want?"

He gazed at her a moment before answering. "Isn't it obvious what I want?" His voice was low, male. "I want some more, sweetness."

She glared at him, incredulous. "I don't know what you're talking about."

"Shall I explain it to you?"

"No!" she said with an explosion of anguish. This can't be happening! Randy thought, averting her eyes from his slow, insinuating smile. It wasn't fair! She'd made one mistake and now she was going to have to pay for it the rest of her life?

She touched her temple, which was already throbbing with the promise of another tension headache. She'd been out of her mind with heartbreak that night. Otherwise, she would never have done the things she'd done—starting with getting on the back of a stranger's motorcycle. Maybe if she hadn't been jilted by her fiancé, maybe if she hadn't been so distraught, it wouldn't have happened. She wouldn't have been on that road late at night, stumbling around in her wedding dress, an open bottle of champagne in her hand. But it had happened—

"That's my price to find your fiancé," he said, cutting

into her thoughts. "I want another night. One night, *all* night, just you and me."

"What is this? Blackmail?"

"Don't be absurd." His voice flared with heat. "If money was the object, we'd have settled this thing when you walked in the door. You blew into my life like a beautiful cyclone, Randy. You shook me up good, and then you disappeared without even saying good-bye. I told myself if I ever ran across you again, I'd teach you some manners. I should be able to do that in one night, don't you think?"

She kept waiting for that spark of amusement to light his eyes, the signal that told her he was playing, baiting her. But it didn't come. His probing gaze drew up sensations she hadn't felt in years, *not since she was last with him*. He was serious, she realized. He meant to hold her hostage for a night of sex. He meant to wreck her life!

"You're the one who's absurd," she cried. "I wouldn't spend the night with you under any circumstances. The man who's missing is my *fiancé*. I'm engaged to be married."

"Married to a man you don't love."

He said the words with such conviction that Randy was startled. "What do you know about my relationship with Hugh?" she demanded.

"All I know is you fell apart in my arms that night. You said love had destroyed your mother, and you'd never let a man do that to you. You told me you'd been jilted by some guy you thought was Prince Charming, and the only way to win with men was to keep them guessing. You swore you'd never marry for love." He hesitated, drawing in a breath. "*And then you seduced me.*"

"I did no such thing!" Randy tried her best to stare him down. She would have loved nothing better than to vaporize him on the spot, to reduce him to a heap of ashes.

But he only crossed his arms, leaned against the wall behind him, and gazed at her with the casual assurance of a man who knew—and approved of—every shameful little secret she had.

"I did not seduce you, dammit," she whispered as if fearing someone might overhear them. "My hands slipped! And no wonder, the reckless way you drove that damn motorcycle! You had me perched on the back, hanging on for dear life. What was I supposed to do with my hands? *Where was I supposed to put them?*"

He drew his thumb back and forth across his chin as if scratching an itch. "You found the right place, darlin'. Don't ever let anybody tell you you aren't good with your hands. You're an artist."

"And you're a bastard," she breathed. "Why are you doing this to me? It was ten years ago. I'm not that person anymore. I never was that person! I don't know what happened to me that night." She clenched her fists, but her voice was almost pleading with him to understand. "I *hate* motorcycles!"

"You didn't appear reluctant to take a ride on mine."

"I *was* reluctant. I don't know why I did it!"

"I've got a pretty good idea."

"Don't say it!" She held up her hand, her eyes colliding with his, sparks flying. But Randy had no intention of backing down this time. There was too much at risk. "I was distraught that night," she insisted, forcing out the words.

He lifted a shoulder. "Okay . . . have it your way."

"What does that mean?"

"It means you're lucky I'm a boy scout. Otherwise, this could be the blackmail you accused me of. I've got plenty on you, sweetness, all of it amazing." After a pregnant pause he pushed off the wall as though intending to leave. "But it isn't blackmail. I haven't sunk to that, yet. It's pretty clear you don't want to deal on my terms, so we don't have a deal. If you change your mind, you know where to find me."

Once again Randy watched Geoff Dias make an exit, this time out of his own office. She followed him to the door as he pushed it open and strode toward a vintage black Porsche parked at the curb. Within seconds he'd tucked his oversize frame into the driver's seat, keyed the ignition, and driven out of her life.

Randy didn't know whether to be relieved or angry. Everything he did provoked her, even the way he'd just let her off the hook. Boy scout? If he was a boy scout, then Attila the Hun must have been his den mother.

Not knowing what else to do, she left his office. But as she started for her own car, she noticed the motorcycle he'd ridden the day before. It was parked in a stall between his office and the gym. She hesitated, feeling weak at the knees and hating the way her heart was knocking. The machine brought back so many memories, all of them frighteningly vivid. And all of them hot enough to make her want to spend the rest of her life in a cold shower.

She approached the stall slowly, coming to a halt as soon as she got close enough to see what was painted on the bike's gas tank. Emblazoned in hot pink was a broken valentine's heart and just beneath it were the words SURRENDER BABY.

If Randy had been clinging to a slender thread of hope that Geoff Dias wasn't really her beautiful drifter, that thread had just snapped.

Geoff wound the Porsche down through its gears, reining in the surging car as he took the freeway exit that spilled into the foothills of the Santa Monica mountains. The whine and grind of harnessed horsepower brought a stirring of satisfaction to his soul. It felt almost as good as the quivering responsiveness of the gearstick under his hand.

He still got off on power and performance. There weren't too many things that did it for him anymore.

But powerful things, they interested him. More than that, he liked exercising the control that came with mastering power. Maybe that's why *she* interested him. He'd meant it when he'd called her a pistol. He'd never met a hotter female, in every sense of the word. Her pain was as fiery as her passion.

Something hit the windshield with a crack, distracting him. It sounded like a rock, but all he could see was a huge tumbleweed rolling down the street straight at him. He cranked the wheel hard, swerving to miss it. The Porsche shuddered and squealed, leaving streaks on the asphalt before he got the car straightened out.

The devil winds were blowing again today, he realized, checking out the hilly terrain around him. Hot gusting Santa Anas moaned in the sycamores and whooshed through the car's open windows, whipping at his hair. The air was saturated with the dense smells of sage, laurel, and road dust.

Moments later he was traversing the narrow road that snaked toward his small house in the backwoods of Coldwater Canyon. As he took the curves, he was aware of another scent, her perfume still clinging to his sweatshirt. It was a hot fragrance, earthy and spicy, redolent of cloves.

Yes, she did interest him.

He turned the sports car into his gravel driveway and let himself out, stretching to his full height and working the kinks out of his muscles. The wind pulled at his clothing as he walked to the ranch-style house he'd bought after leaving the Pentagon several years ago. He'd had two partners in those days, both of whom he'd met in the Marines. He and Johnny Starhawk had been recruited into the Pentagon's Recovery Operations Unit by Chase Beaudine, their job description being to free American hostages and POWs. The three of them had quickly made international headlines with their exploits. Geoff still carried a snapshot in his wallet of their celebration in a Greek taverna after their first successful mission. Chase and Johnny had both had the sense to retire after a few years and take up normal lives. Geoff was the only one still playing soldier.

A stack of mail was piled up under the slot as he let himself into the house. Noticing a pale blue engraved envelope on top, he knelt and tore it open. His lips curved into a smile as he read the invitation to an anniversary party for Johnny Starhawk. Johnny and his wife, Honor, had been married a year.

"One year?" Geoff's laughter was husky with affection. "And that crazy SOB thought it wouldn't last. Good for you, Johnny."

Crouched there, gazing at the invitation, Geoff was revisited by memories of both his former partners. Johnny had been a wild man in the Marines, driven by some inner rage none of his buddies understood, or dared ask about. Irish-Apache by birth, he had intuitive instincts and tracking abilities that had made him invaluable in recovery operations, but it was his keen intelligence, his analytical brilliance, that had ultimately led him to the career he'd been born for.

Geoff wasn't at all surprised that Johnny had become a high-powered attorney, but a happily married man? That did surprise him, especially since Johnny's golden-girl bride had been the source of most of his rage. She'd betrayed him when they were young, and Johnny wasn't a forgiving soul.

Geoff fingered the invitation and smiled. He almost wished he could go to the party and see how they were doing. He'd had some firsthand experience with the volatile reconciliation that had led to their marriage. As far as he knew, no two people had had more reason to be together—or more heartbreak keeping them apart.

As for Chase Beaudine, the hell-bent Marine who'd recruited Geoff into recovery operations, he was as thoroughly roped and hog-tied as a man could be these days. He had a couple of kids already and was turning his small cabin in the Wyoming foothills into a ranch.

His redheaded wife, Annie, a tiny woman with a huge spirit, was the perfect match for a hard case like Beaudine.

Geoff dropped the invitation back on the pile. A stab of something that must have been loneliness hit him as he thought about his two buddies, how they'd changed, how full and complete their lives must be now. He was happy for them, but maybe he was a little envious too.

A tall can of beer from the refrigerator went a long way toward easing his pain. By the time he'd finished it, he wasn't thinking about Chase and Johnny anymore. His mind had returned to its more recent preoccupation. Randy.

He helped himself to another can of beer, then leaned against the closed refrigerator door, rubbing his thumb over the can's condensation as he contemplated the mystery she presented. Women weren't supposed to seduce men and disappear, that was a male thing. But it wasn't just her knack for breathless seduction that made her so unforgettable. There was all the rest of it—the tears, the vulnerability, the way she clung to him, tucking her face into the hollow of his shoulder, making him want to ache with her heartrending sobs. She'd changed moods with dizzying speed that night, pounding on his chest one minute and railing at him for the sins of all men, and then before he could catch his balance, she was kissing him with more whimpering hunger and raw need than he'd ever known from a woman.

Hell, yes, he was interested.

He popped the beer can's top and took a swig of the ice-cold brew, hardly tasting it. What man wouldn't be interested in a beautiful woman who hit him like a cyclone and left him confused and gasping for air?

A drop of sweat trickled down his forehead, and he wiped the moisture away, feeling the afternoon heat rise and thicken around him. It was going to be a hellacious night. The devil winds always kicked the thermometer up into the nineties, even in February. One of these years he'd have to get air-conditioning.

He stripped off his threadbare sweatshirt with his free hand and tossed it as he strolled out of the kitchen. The garment landed on the hand-carved molding of the antique grandfather clock that had been passed down through his father's side of the family. It was the only thing he wanted from his parents' estate after their deaths. And sometimes, when the chimes rang out, he wished he hadn't taken it. The sound was so damn forlorn.

Needing to clear his thoughts, he walked through the cluttered living room and down the hallway toward the back porch sunroom he'd converted into a workout space. All distractions vanished when he entered the stark, monasterylike environment, all thoughts of the past, of women and sex. This was where he mastered errant impulses, anything that didn't feed the source of his mental and physical powers. This was where he harnessed his own will.

He stopped at the doorway long enough to set down the can of beer and remove his shoes before he stepped onto the braided hemp carpet. The room was bare of furnishings except for a low table holding an oriental board game of black and white stones and a two-inch metallic sphere suspended from the ceiling on a thin rope. The objects were meant to teach mental detachment and to train the intuition. A solid oak support beam stood in the center of the room.

Geoff walked across the coarse hemp slowly, honing his concentration, gathering energy in the pit of his stomach. The oak beam was his sparring partner. It had broken his foot once, shattering countless bones. Over the years it had bruised and beaten him into submission until he'd found the part of himself that was the beam. Once he had mastered that part of himself, he'd mastered the beam.

Surrender, baby, he thought softly.

He stood very still, gazing at the beam until it appeared to move and undulate before his eyes. Feeding on the wood's energy, he drew it into himself until the corresponding energy in the pit of his stomach imploded and surged through him.

With a hissing sound, he leaped, whirled, and kicked, striking out savagely with his bare foot. A shock wave slammed through his body as he connected with the solid oak. He knew instantly that he'd hit wrong, with the top of his foot instead of the blade. The pain that shot up his leg was staggering, blinding.

He dropped to his knees, letting the sharp throbs pierce him, willing himself to become the pain so that he could master it. There was no question in his mind what had gone wrong. His focus wasn't perfectly honed. He wasn't clear. He had freed himself of every conscious distraction except one. Her.

The seductress in a virginal white wedding gown.

She'd haunted his mind ever since that night. She was the one thing that he, who'd devoted his life to self-mastery, hadn't been able to master. And the way she'd come back into his life, through a missing-persons ad to find her fiancé, was too dark an irony to be ignored.

It had been years since he'd seen her in the flesh, but now that he'd found her again, he wasn't going to be diverted. He had something in mind for Miranda Witherspoon, the blushing bride-to-be. Something befitting the occasion.

A moment later he was on his feet, concentrating energy, gathering the storm inside him and locating its center, the eye of perfect stillness. A sound hissed through his teeth, snakelike. He kicked the post again, several times, perfectly, powerfully. As he felt the energy from his body reverberate through the wood, returning to its origins, a smile crossed his face. He was ready.

•   •   •

Randy pressed the button on her intercom. "Did that last applicant leave yet?" she asked as Barb picked up the phone. They both knew who she was referring to. The mercenary she'd just interviewed could have been an escapee from San Quentin's death row.

"Only after I threatened to call in the military police," Barb snapped. "Will you please stop interviewing these psychos, Randy? You're endangering both our lives."

"What choice do I have, Barb? Hugh's lost somewhere in South America and no one seems to care but me." But Randy's pleading tone did nothing to mollify her assistant.

"You've already called the FBI, the State Department, the local police in Rio, and the consulate," Barb pointed out. "They're the experts on these things, for heaven's sake. Why don't you let them do their job?"

"I only wish they would. My wedding is two weeks away!"

"Well, just tell me one thing," Barb shot back. "Are we doing this again tomorrow? Are we *interviewing*, Randy? Because if we are, I'm wearing a bullet-proof vest and crash helmet."

"I didn't know you had a bullet-proof vest."

"Randy!"

"Sorry, I was just trying to imagine it with your gold jewelry." Randy winced as the receiver banged down. She rose from her chair, determined to find a replacement for Geoff Dias. She'd seen four applicants before noon, one of them an ex-priest who had seemed promising until she learned he was allergic to his own perspiration and had to avoid humid climates. The applicants she'd met after lunch had seemed more interested in replacing her fiancé than in finding him. The last one had insinuated he could make her forget about Hugh in ten seconds flat if she'd sit on his lap and play horsey.

Maybe it was the Santa Ana winds, she thought, walking to her desk and picking up a framed picture of her and Hugh. Everyone got a little weird when the devil winds blew in. She traced the scrollwork on the antique silver frame with her fingers, touching the faint smile on her fiancé's lean, bespectacled face. Hugh was such a serious man. Some even called him cheerless, but she'd never minded that about him. She'd always admired his drive, his single-minded desire to succeed. Everyone said they were an ideal match.

Hugh Hargrove, she thought, where are you? Your timing stinks. Disappearing three weeks before your own wedding!

Tears filled her eyes as she set the picture down. She was being unforgivably selfish, worrying about weddings when Hugh's safety was in question. She ought to be pining for him, like any other fiancée would. But she'd never loved Hugh in that silly, senseless way that people do when the attraction is primarily physical. She'd never wanted to love a man that way.

Her mother's relationships had cured her of any desire for a grand passion. Edna was always caught up in some devastating physical attraction or other, and all it had gotten her for her trouble was a string of tragic affairs with men who caroused and couldn't commit to anything but their own selfish needs. Randy had been devoted to her mother. She'd loved Edna dearly, but she'd promised herself she would not repeat Edna's mistakes. She would never let a man become everything in her life, especially a dishonorable man.

Randy's intercom buzzed rudely. She picked up the phone to hear Barb announce that it was quitting time and she was leaving for the day. "Just so you know," Barb said ominously. "I'm updating my resume."

Randy decided not to take the threat seriously as the phone clicked in her ear yet again. Barb had a dramatic nature. She was always mumbling and grumbling about something. Secretly, Randy was sympathetic to her assistant's concerns. The thought of even one more interview appalled her too.

Perhaps she should make the trip to Rio by herself.

As she sat down at her desk to clear up some priority items, that idea began to take on more appeal. Carlos Santeras, the man Hugh was last reported seen with, lived somewhere in the hills that bordered the city of Rio. It wasn't as if she would have to trek through the jungle if she decided to pay him a visit; she could just make some discreet inquiries. At least she'd be down there instead of sitting helplessly behind a desk!

An hour later Randy was locking up to go home. The dimmed lights in executive row told her she was the last to leave as she made her way down the hall to the elevator. She rolled one shoulder and then the other, loosening tight muscles. The last few days had been exhausting, and she was running out of strings to pull to find Hugh.

The express elevator came and took her down to the subterranean parking garage. As the doors swooshed open, she stepped out absently, then hesitated. A sound that resembled laughter alerted her that someone was there.

"Who is it?" she asked an instant before spotting him. The large, shaggy-haired man who moved out of the shadows was the last mercenary she'd interviewed. "What do you want?" she asked.

He walked toward her, making a strange rattling sound that might have been laughter. It was hard to tell because he wasn't smiling. But Randy didn't have to ask her question a second time. It was obvious what he wanted by the malevolent gleam that lit his eyes. She stepped back into the elevator and jabbed the DOOR CLOSE button.

He rushed the door and jammed it with his body.

"Help!" Randy screamed as he caught hold of her arm and hauled her toward him. She jerked back frantically, kicking at him and trying to press the button at the same time.

"Let go!" she screamed, hitting him sharply in the shin.

"Come here," he snarled, dragging her into his arms. The alcohol on his breath choked her as he plastered her against his massive body. He locked a beefy arm around her neck and jerked her head back, paralyzing her as he ripped out the neckline of her blouse. Randy screamed as seams popped and buttons went flying.

"Stop!" she gasped as he tightened the armlock. He was cutting off her breathing. She was going to black out! Her vision went spotty, static dancing wildly in her head, and her legs folded, sagging together.

She was slipping into unconsciousness as her attacker let out a roar of pain, then lurched forward. Randy was too weak to stop him as he tumbled into the elevator on top of her. They both crashed to the floor, the impact of his dead weight knocking the wind out of her.

Dazed, she saw the elevator doors close, sealing off her only route of escape. She struggled to get out from under him, but she couldn't move. She was locked in the elevator with him! Her terrified shriek bounced off the walls.

Four

Randy twisted and shoved, struggling in vain to push the mercenary's weight off her. Panic gripped her as she searched for some way to get free. He appeared to have been knocked unconscious, but he was beginning to stir. His soft moans told her he was waking up.

She spotted her purse and grasped for it, thinking to use it as a weapon. But as her fingers touched the chain strap, the elevator doors flew open and Geoff Dias surged inside. He dragged the man off her, slammed him up against the elevator wall, and reared back to hit him.

Geoff's fist stopped in midair as the man slumped forward, seemingly out cold. Geoff considered the mercenary's bobbing head and slack jaw for an instant, then released him and stepped back, letting him slide to the floor.

Randy struggled to get up, but before she'd made it to her feet, Geoff was pressing a button that would send the elevator rocketing to the top floor. "Let's go!" he said, catching hold of her and pulling her with him through the closing doors.

They rushed through the gloom of the garage, past Randy's car, and up the ramp that would take them to the street level. Randy was thoroughly winded by the time they reached Geoff's motorcycle and too dazed to protest when he lifted her up and settled her on the bike's passenger seat.

He swung onto the bike, twisted the key, and stomped the kick start, but even the roar of the powerful engine couldn't startle Randy out of her dazed state. They'd gone several blocks before she was clearheaded enough to fully comprehend what was happening. *Geoff Dias had just rescued her and now she was flying off into the dark heart of the night with him on his motorcycle.*

She hated motorcycles! But there was no way to remind him of that now. He was going much too fast, and the wind was whistling so loudly in her ears, she couldn't have made herself heard anyway. She knew they must be breaking several laws—the speed limit for one, the helmet law for another, but she couldn't concern herself with that now. Her first priority was staying alive, she told herself, which meant hanging on and praying.

She clutched him tighter and ducked her head down, burrowing into the shelter of his powerful shoulder blades. His long blond hair flew around her like a protective cloak. She hadn't had any reason to be grateful for his size before, but right now she was glad he was a big man. He felt reassuringly strong and warm, and she actually allowed herself to relax for a moment, to trust that he would deliver her safely to wherever they were going.

It was an odd feeling, trusting a man. She didn't plan to indulge the sentiment long. Especially with a man like Geoff, who was too much like the men who came and went in her mother's life. Randy had often wondered if witnessing Edna's romantic disasters had left her incapable of trusting the male gender. She'd thought she trusted her fiancé completely, but her suspicions about Hugh's fidelity had been immediately aroused when he hadn't returned as planned from Brazil.

A horn blared and Randy gripped Geoff tighter, forgetting all about moral dilemmas. They shot through an intersection, and the bright lights and crowded streets reminded her that her predicament was more than merely life-threatening. It was *embarrassing*. Her skirt had crawled up so high, the control top of her pantyhose was showing, her blouse was ripped open, her collar was flapping in the breeze, and she was wrapped around Geoff Dias like a Band-Aid on a blister.

The bike tilted suddenly, arcing into a curve. Randy closed her eyes, astonished at the torque of the huge machine and the strength of the G forces pressing down on them. It felt as if Geoff were going to lay them out on their sides. Images of tumbling bodies and bloody, broken limbs screened through her mind. But a moment later they'd come out of the turn, straightened, and were whooshing into the darkness again.

He'd gone off the beaten track, Randy realized, looking around her. They were on a road that was largely residential and very quiet at this time of night. As he slowed the bike down, she became aware of how deeply her fingers were digging into his flesh. He was wearing a T-shirt, but she could feel the tension in his stomach muscles, the heat and resilience.

She relaxed her hold, aware of vibrations in her fingertips. Was it his body quivering? Or hers? The warm, tingly sensations buzzed in other, more sensitive places as well, such as the part of her anatomy she was sitting on. She could see where a long ride on one of these machines might be quite stimulating. Perhaps that explained what had happened to her the last time she'd been on a motorcycle behind him. Somehow in that night's wild ride, she'd found her hands in an area much more dangerous than his ridged stomach. But how she got her hands all the way down there she still didn't know.

He would probably say she did it intentionally, that she was looking for forbidden thrills. And considering the other things she'd done with him that night, a jury would undoubtedly have agreed with him. But Randy was convinced some dark force had taken possession of her will that night. From childhood she'd been haunted by the fear that a destructive impulse was lying in wait to prove to her that no matter how hard she tried to fight it, she really was a bad girl, a pushover for a handsome scoundrel, just like Edna.

"What are you doing?" Geoff yelled back at her, gunning the engine as they headed for a steep hill. "Hang on!"

Randy hadn't realized she'd let go. She grabbed hold of him as the bike surged upward, clinging to great handfuls of his cotton T-shirt and fighting to anchor herself.

"Hang on to *me*," he shouted. "Unless you're trying to rip my shirt off. In which case, help yourself."

She clamped her hands to his midsection and glued her body to his, hugging him with her thighs as they shot over the crest of the hill, went airborne, and literally flew down the other side. There was no way to avoid gluing herself to him! It was that or get thrown off the bike.

They landed with a resounding thud halfway down the hill. But it wasn't until they'd swooped to the bottom and leveled out that Randy realized her fingers had worked their way inside one of several large holes in his T-shirt. He was perspiring lightly, and the feel of his moist, bare skin sent her mind reeling back again to that other time when her hands slipped.

When she'd first realized what part of him she was touching that night, she'd jerked her hands away. But by then it was too late. Her senses had been awakened, her imagination aroused. Excitement had streamed through her in a quivering current, galvanizing her like an electrical shock.

Before she knew it, she'd been touching him there again, perhaps even caressing him, fascinated by the heat and hardness pouring out of him, by the havoc she could wreak with her hands. She hadn't been able to control herself. And then he'd lost control too. He'd found a dark place to park the bike, and he'd taken over from there—

A dark place? "Stop!" she cried out as Geoff turned off onto an even more isolated street. "Where are you taking me? What are you doing?"

He slowed down the bike and glanced over his shoulder. "Unless something's changed," he said wryly, "I'm rescuing you from the bad guy."

"Oh . . . yes, right. And don't think I'm not grateful," she assured him, wondering if it was safe to let go of him now. The memories of how magnificently aroused he'd become that night, of what they'd done in the dark alley where he'd pulled the bike, were whirling in her mind.

"Are we going to stop anytime soon?" she asked him breathlessly. "I'm sure he's not following us, and I'd like a moment to collect myself." *And get off this rolling vibrator.*

He pulled the bike over to the curb and cut the engine. He'd stopped by the playground of a school yard, and in the sudden silence Randy's hearing sharpened. The playground was deserted, but she could discern the soft creaking of the swings in the night breezes. The sounds sent a strange rush of longing through her. As a child living in a musty and depressingly tiny walk-up, she'd fantasized about a house with a backyard and a swing set. Somehow those things had signified a normal life, with all the love and security of a close-knit family. At times the yearning had been so acute, she'd stolen into more affluent neighborhoods and watched the children at play, imagining she was one of them.

As she gazed at the playground, Randy sensed Geoff Dias was staring at her. He'd twisted around on the bike and was studying her as if he understood about backyards and swing sets, maybe even about yearning. She returned his gaze for a moment, surprised. It was the first time she'd ever thought of him in that way, as having a childhood.

He'd always seemed like some dark and sinister figment of her imagination, not a real man, but a demon sent to test her. If everyone had a day of reckoning in their lives, a moment of coming to terms with the past, then Geoff Dias was her day of reckoning. She could almost believe that he was her destructive impulse come to life, destined to prove her unworthy, to remind her where she'd come from, what she'd been.

And yet now he was gazing at her with curiosity, perhaps even some small measure of sympathy.

"You remind me of someone," he remarked, idly touching the torn silk of her collar, taking it between his fingers.

"I do?"

He drew the silk over her lips, as if he could banish the slight droop at each corner of her mouth. "You look like the gypsy bride in white lace who got on the back of my bike one night. She was sad too."

His voice felt like a physical touch. The huskiness seemed to slide over her skin, a feathery pressure. It made her shiver inside and wonder about him. Why had he gone to so much trouble to track her down? With another man she would have chalked it up to male ego. But Geoff Dias didn't look like the sort who needed to use women to prove his virility.

Still, the words emblazoned on his motorcycle spoke volumes. They said he was an incorrigible rogue and womanizer. Even now his gaze was drifting to the gaping neckline of her blouse where her heart was beating furiously and her breasts were spilling out of her scanty bra. She must have looked a sight with her blouse hanging off her shoulder and her skirt hiked up. Just the sort of sight he undoubtedly liked, by the way he was slowly undressing her with his eyes, removing what little clothing she had left.

Her flesh shivered and swelled, responding as if out of some biological instinct, a leaf opening to the light. She breathed in deeply, loving the feeling, hating it because it made her feel so weak.

"I wasn't sad," she countered, determined to distract him as much as to explain. "I was heartbroken. I was out of my mind that night. I never would have done those things if the circumstances had been different. You must know that."

"I don't know what you would have done. I only know what you did." The strip of silk he'd been holding fluttered down her throat and landed on her breast. He reclaimed it, his fingers loitering, softly violating her bare skin. "We both know what you did, sweetness."

She flushed hotly and looked away. Now she understood what he liked about her, why he'd come back. . . . *He thought she was easy.*

Deep inside her, the shivery sensations increased, fanning out like ripples over water. Why did he make her feel this way? So weak inside, so loose? Why was she so quick to respond to him? She clutched the strip of silk, trying to pull it out of his hands, but he tugged back, releasing it only when she looked up and met his eyes.

"I'm not what you think," she said.

His gaze darkened, contradicting her. "Oh, *baby*—" He laughed softly, drawing the husky words out until they all but curled up and sighed. "I hope you're wrong about that. Because I like what I think you are."

She wanted to defend herself, but it wouldn't have done any good. He knew her fatal flaw. He'd seen the wild streak that no one else even knew existed, certainly not Hugh.

Suddenly his hair caught the moonlight, flaming in the darkness as he tilted his head. "When do we leave?" he asked, swinging his leg over the handlebars and sliding off the bike.

"Leave?"

"For Brazil. I'm going with you."

"You are?"

His T-shirt was hanging out of his fatigue pants. He tucked it back in and glanced up at her. "Any objections?"

She could think of several hundred, but she didn't dare voice them if she wanted to find her fiancé. "What made you change your mind?"

"The thug who attacked you," he said, indicating her ripped clothing and disheveled appearance. He reached around her and straightened her blouse, drawing it up on her shoulders, his hands warming her through the material. And then they closed gently on her shoulders, drawing her forward.

Randy glanced up at him, her heart rocketing as she realized what was happening. He was going to kiss her. But not roughly, not wildly. This wasn't a surprise attack where he whipped her around, pressed her against a wall, and held her prisoner with his body until she surrendered. This would be slow and terribly sweet, a melting kiss.

Somehow she knew all that without question. She also knew she should hold him off. At the very least she should turn her head away! But she didn't do either of those things. Instead, she found herself leaning into his hands and tilting up her chin to meet him halfway. Dear God, she *was* easy. Look at her! She couldn't even find the strength of will to stop a kiss when she saw it coming. What would happen when he—

All other thoughts flew out of her head as his lips touched hers. She choked back a moan, but she couldn't stop the trembling that swept her or the shivery lights swirling deep inside her. Why did it feel so wonderful when he did these things to her?

The sudden warmth of his hand on her face ignited a sweet burning that crept into her throat and filled her mouth. He stroked and played with her face as though it were a baby's, caressing her with his surprisingly sensual fingers, breathing soft air through her parted teeth. Lord, what he did to her! The ache in her throat was so powerful she couldn't even swallow. She opened her mouth to him, whimpering softly, pleading for something she shouldn't even have been thinking about.

She felt him tremble and hesitate. His hands contracted on her shoulders, tightening as if he couldn't make up his mind what to do with her. "I'm taking you to Rio, sweetness," he said roughly, almost possessively, pulling her back to give her that news. "You won't be safe with anyone else."

"Are you saying I'll be safe with you?" she asked him.

"No, I'm not saying that. But I can promise you one thing."

"What's that?"

"We will find your fiancé."

"We will? How do you know that?"

"Because I'm going to bring the bastard back—if only to prove to you that you don't want him back."

"But I do—" The protest died on her lips.

He tipped her chin up, and she swallowed the breath she was taking. She strained toward him instinctively, shameless in her excitement. But apparently Geoff Dias had no intention of giving her what she wanted, which was another sweet, sinful kiss. Instead, he stroked the rough stubble of his five o'clock shadow over her baby-soft cheeks, abrading her skin. Instead, he touched his hot tongue to the lobe of her ear and whispered terrible, terrible things into that delicate orifice. Shocking things that made the shivery lights in her belly burn painfully bright.

"It's all coming back to you, isn't it, Randy?" he

murmured. "You're starting to remember how it was . . . with us."

"I remember," she breathed, her head beginning to swirl in concert with the sensations inside her. Why did she allow him to say the things he said to her? To do the things he did? She wasn't anybody's pushover, dammit. Any other man would have taken such liberties at risk of his life, but Geoff Dias did pretty much whatever he pleased, no matter how outrageous.

And she allowed it. Invited it, if she was being truthful. Sins of the flesh, she thought, shuddering. She had probably committed almost all of them with Geoff Dias in just one unforgettable night. Maybe they'd even invented a few. Was that why she couldn't find the strength to stop him now? Because he'd done all this to her and much, much more? *Because she knew how good a man he was?*

"How safe do you feel now, Randy?" he asked, feathering the fine hair that was curling damply to her temple.

"Not very safe at all."

He smiled knowingly and released her, remounting the bike. As he twisted the ignition key he glanced over his shoulder at her. "Feels good, doesn't it?"

The bike jerked forward and Randy grabbed hold of his vest. This can't be happening, she told herself as the powerful vibrations of the revving engine surged through her. She was on the back of a massive motorcycle with a man she'd had the appalling judgment to have a forbidden fling with ten years ago. A mysterious drifter. A veritable stranger! And now fate had arranged it so he was the only man who would or could take her into the wilds of Brazil to find her financé.

A thin, hysterical giggle slipped from her throat as she buried her head in Geoff Dias's back. *This can't be happening.*

By the next morning Randy had lost her sense of humor and regained her sanity. Perhaps it was the cold whites and grays of the international airline terminal that sobered her up as she waited for Geoff Dias to arrive for their flight to Brazil. More likely it was the sleepless night she'd spent convincing herself that finding Hugh was the most important thing in her life, and nothing could deter her. She could handle *ten* like Geoff Dias if that's what it would take to accomplish her goal.

Cooler heads will prevail, she promised herself, staring out the terminal windows at the huge 747 they would soon be boarding. At least *her* head would be cool. That's what had brought her this far in life, and it would get her wherever else she needed to go. She hadn't devoted her entire adult existence to improving her situation just to throw it all away for another fling with a rogue on a motorcycle.

Ignoring the dull throb above her right eye, she smoothed the lapel of her sand-washed silk jumpsuit. She would need nerves of space-age steel to keep Geoff Dias in line. Still, it could be done. And *she* could do it. She'd done everything else in life she'd put her mind to, hadn't she?

And he was, after all, just a man. . . .

"I dreamt about you last night."

The husky male voice seemed to breathe the words into her consciousness. Geoff Dias had come up behind her, and the sensation that washed over Randy was as much weakness as surprise. The rigidity in her spine began to topple like a row of dominoes, vertebrae loosening all the way to her tailbone. She could feel his presence everywhere. He was as close to her, as enveloping, as if he'd slipped his arms around her waist, and yet he wasn't touching her.

"I hope it was in color," she said, congratulating herself on how nonchalant she sounded.

She turned around to a pair of mirrored sunglasses identical to the ones she'd stared into a decade ago. They flashed with the dazzling light from the windows, hurting her eyes. For a second she was transfixed by her own startled reflection, and then by the certainty that this man must surely be the personification of her worst fears, a demon sent to test her.

"Technicolor," he said. "With Dolby stereo."

"I prefer Sensurround. How did it end?"

"He got the girl."

"Too pat." Randy knew by his smile that she'd scored a point. She was putting up a reasonably good fight so far, blocking his advances, returning his jabs. But as she bent to pick up her carry-on, her hands were shaking.

A half hour later they were in the air and soaring toward Miami, their first connection in the long flight to Rio. The throbbing above Randy's eye had worsened. Not only was she crowded in a tiny airplane seat between Geoff Dias and the window, but she was faced with an unnerving task. They had never discussed the "price" for his services since that day in his office. She wanted to believe he wouldn't hold her to that bargain, but she couldn't take anything for granted with a man like him. She had hired him, in a manner of speaking, and the form of payment had to be discussed.

He was drawing something when she turned to him, sketching what looked like the outlines of a face on his drink napkin. She couldn't quite make out what it was. "I'm willing to pay you what I promised," she said. "Twice your normal fee."

He didn't look up. "Keep your money. You can't afford me."

Randy was tempted to let it go at that, but she didn't want any surprises down the line. "If you don't want to be paid, why are you doing this, out of the goodness of your heart? I didn't know mercenaries did pro bono work."

He set the pencil down and reached into an inner pocket of his vest. "I told you why," he said, drawing out a snapshot she'd given him of Hugh. "I'm going to bring

Mr. Fortune Five Hundred back alive so you can take a good long look at his Armani suits and his little round glasses and quit kidding yourself. You don't want pinstripes, Randy. You'd be bored silly."

And who do I want, Mr. God's Gift? Mr. Holes-in-Your-Pants Mercenary? You? Randy curbed the impulse to voice the question. Wisely, she didn't bring up his "price" again either. He hadn't mentioned it, and she would leave it that way. As for not wanting Hugh back, Geoff Dias couldn't have been more wrong. By the time they found her fiancé, she was going to convince the golden one next to her that she was in love with Hugh and totally committed to him.

She rubbed her forehead, wincing as she touched tense muscles and tender nerves.

"PMS?" Geoff asked, smiling faintly.

"Headache," she muttered, closing her eyes and settling back in the seat. "I'll be fine. I have a relaxation technique that relieves the tension."

"This might be quicker." He drew the silver flask from his vest and offered it to her.

Randy flinched back. "Not if I were dying of thirst in the desert! What is that stuff?"

"Two parts Gatoraid, one part Tang." He grinned. "Hey, if it's good enough for the astronauts . . ."

Randy settled back and closed her eyes again, pointedly ignoring him as she concentrated on relaxing the muscles in her scalp and neck. She would have guessed the drink was an exotic love potion from the jungle, designed to turn women into glassy-eyed nymphomaniacs. At least he had a sense of humor.

When she opened her eyes a short time later, Geoff was still preoccupied with his sketch, and she was pleased to know he could entertain himself. Maybe this trip wasn't going to be such an ordeal after all, she decided, pulling a magazine from the pocket on the chair in front of her. She leafed through it, coming to an article on Rio.

"Did you know that Rio de Janeiro means 'River of January'?" she asked him. "It was named in 1502 by the Portuguese sea captain who discovered it. That's beautiful, don't you think?"

He glanced up, studying her features, gazing at the line of her jaw, the arc of her eyebrows, her mouth. "Yeah, beautiful."

She smiled, surprised by the compliment, and pleased.

He resumed sketching almost immediately, and though Randy tried to get a look at what he was doing, she still couldn't make it out. Spurred on by his praise, she felt compelled to talk to him. Maybe she could make him understand how important this trip was to her. She wanted him to know how her life had changed since she'd been with him, and how her relationship with Hugh symbolized that change.

"You know I'm a West Side kid. I grew up in a neighborhood not far from your office."

"Ummm," he murmured, "rough part of town."

"It was," she admitted, realizing she'd never shared the darker details of her childhood with anyone, not even Hugh. "My mother raised me by herself. She had to work all hours—two, sometimes three, jobs."

"Looks like she did all right by you."

He glanced at her briefly, something that might have been admiration lurking in his expression.

"Well, that's just it," Randy said, encouraged to go on. "Edna had these dreams she was never able to make come true, about how the perfect man would show up one day and sweep us both away and change our lives."

"Sounds like Cinderella stuff," he said, not unkindly.

"Yes, it was, but she believed it completely."

As Geoff continued to sketch, Randy found herself opening up even more. She confided the harsh realities of her childhood, the men who came and went in Edna's life, her mother's illness, and their increasingly sordid existence. "I promised myself I'd do things differently, that I'd make something of my life," she told him, her voice softening as she hesitated. "Hugh Hargrove is part of that something."

The pencil went still in Geoff's hand. "Do you love him?" he asked.

"Yes . . . in my way, I do. He really is the perfect man for me. Prince Charming in the flesh, Edna would have said. Maybe that's as close as anyone ever gets to love."

Geoff made a series of quick slashes with the pencil, then handed the napkin to her. "Perfection has nothing to do with love, Randy."

She stared at what he'd drawn, her throat going dry. "What is this?" she asked, knowing full well. It was a sketch of a young woman's tear-streaked face, and her expression was so full of sweet, wanton yearnings, so hungry for love, that Randy felt exposed just looking at her. The young woman was her, and the sketch had captured her feelings that night with painful clarity. It spoke of the flaring desire she'd felt for a beautiful stranger, and of the incredible pleasure he'd given her.

"I don't know what you feel for this Hargrove character," Geoff said, "but that's what you felt the night we were together."

Randy's head had begun to throb again, but it couldn't compete with the pounding of her heart. The napkin slipped from her fingers, fluttering to the floor.

"I don't want to talk about that night," she said, turning away from him and staring out the window. She tried to focus on the terrain below, the clouds, but she couldn't see anything but that anguished face. Her own face. She barely knew who that young woman was, but she could feel the force of her needs, the depth of her emotion. Those feelings were stirring inside her now, and they frightened her, frightened her badly.

"Please," she said sharply, "don't *ever* bring that night up again."

Five

The woman took no prisoners.

That thought flashed through Geoff's mind more than once as he lounged in a settee in the lobby of a luxurious Rio de Janeiro hotel and watched Randy do battle with the Brazilian reservations clerk. They'd arrived at the hotel a short time ago, only to find that the rooms she'd booked had not been held despite everything she'd done to lock in the reservations. Worse, it was Carnaval in Rio. The hotels were overrun with tourists and revelers come to take in the annual pre-Lenten orgy. There wasn't a room available in the city.

"Go to a *barato*?" Randy cried softly, aghast as the clerk suggested she try the Brazilian equivalent of a flophouse. "I'll camp out in your lobby first! I'm in the hotel business, and I know you have rooms. At the very least you're holding a suite open for emergencies—and this *is* one."

Her voice was hushed but it carried like wind chimes in an icy breeze. What was it they called women like her? Geoff wondered idly. Tough cookies? Brass cupcakes? Just about any combination of steel and softness would do. Her appearance was deceptively feminine, with her supple dancer's build, velvet-black eyes, and equally dark hair. She looked delicate enough to be a Barbie doll, but there had to be cast-iron reinforcements in her backbone.

"No suite," the clerk insisted, his English becoming less intelligible with his agitation. "Es no room leff."

"I meant it when I said I'd camp out in the lobby," Randy warned him, her fingernails clicking on the marble countertop that separated them. "I hope your guests won't mind that I sleep in the nude."

Geoff grinned and settled in, kicking his feet up on the table in front of him. He'd always enjoyed a good fight, and Randy fought good. Back in the good old days when women were property, she would have been the kind of wife a man kept on a short leash. Or tried to, poor jerk. Despite all her attempts at cool professionalism, she was headstrong and willful by nature, which probably had a lot to do with why he was attracted to her. If he'd been her husband, he wouldn't have been foolhardy enough to resort to a leash, but he might not have wanted to let her out of his sight for very long.

"Are you prepared for a scene out of *Nightmare on Elm Street* right here in this lobby?" Randy asked ominously.

The telephone began to jangle and as the harried clerk picked it up, Randy glanced around at Geoff, steely determination written in the bones of her lovely face. Apparently the sight of him stretched out didn't please her greatly. She abandoned her post at the desk and headed his way.

"We may be sleeping on the streets," she said, looking as if she'd like to kick his legs off the table. "You might have the decency to look concerned."

"Decency was never my strong suit."

The way her nostrils flared made Geoff think of a small fierce animal. Everything about her shouted, "Up yours, mister," and that kind of defiance had always stirred his blood. He had the strongest desire to grab her wrist and pull her down on his lap. With her, anger could turn to passion with one hot, steaming kiss. He knew that from experience. Damn near "religious" experience.

"Are you completely devoid of social skills?" she whispered, then shook her head. "Why am I asking? Of course you are. We're in a foreign country, faced with a lodging crisis, and you can't even muster up the energy to help me deal with the reservations clerk."

He cocked a shoulder. "I wouldn't want to cramp your style, sweetness. You're doing fine from where I'm sitting."

"Cramp my style?" she yelped softly, disbelieving. "You couldn't cramp my style on your best day. In fact, grab hold of your pants, Conan, because you haven't seen anything yet." She zapped him with a dark look as if to make sure he got the message, then spun around to resume her duel with the clerk.

Geoff expected fireworks, but instead she walked to the counter and very calmly crooked her finger at the frazzled young man, coaxing him to bend forward so that she could murmur something in his ear. He did, reluctantly, and their whispered conversation went on for several seconds before the clerk snapped his head up and nodded. Randy glanced over at Geoff, a flash of triumph in her eyes.

A moment later she was walking toward Geoff, waggling a room key at him. "Our accommodations are ready."

"Accommodations?"

"Um-hmm," she said, clearly pleased with herself. "We have the presidential suite at our disposal. No charge."

"How did you manage that?"

"I merely mentioned the name of the man we're in town to do business with—Carlos Santeras. I suggested that Carlos might be just the slightest bit put out if he couldn't find us when he came by for our breakfast meeting tomorrow morning."

Geoff did manage to rouse himself for that. "Are you nuts?" he breathed, standing with one whip of his powerful legs.

Randy dropped the key in her blouse pocket, looking all the more pleased for having gotten a rise out of him. "I prefer to think of it as expedient," she said. "Is there a problem? You were admiring my style before, if I remember."

Geoff pulled her aside to impress upon her the dangers of dropping names of local criminals. "You're lucky the clerk didn't call the police," he told her. "Santeras might have hired a public relations firm to clean up his image, but he's still a crook, trust me. He's suspected of running an international smuggling ring— everything from guns to priceless art."

"I'm familiar with Mr. Santeras's reputation, thank you. And I also happen to know that he's buying into resort hotels, which is why he may have had dealings with Hugh. I think they were both bidding on the same chain."

Geoff snorted. "If that's the case, then Hugh-baby is history. Santeras isn't the type to play fair with his competition."

"Hugh . . . history?"

She looked so stricken, Geoff felt a flash of guilt. "Settle down," he said irritably. "I'll track down your fiancé. You'll never know what a colossal mistake you're making unless I find the little weasel and bring him back."

She couldn't seem to decide whether to thank him or argue with him. He ended her dilemma by pointing out a bank of elevators. "Let's check out the room," he suggested.

"Rooms," she hastened to correct. "It's a very large suite, with three bedrooms."

She continued explaining the concept of a suite to

him at length as they rode up in the elevator. Either she wanted to impress upon him the vast size of the place, which meant plenty of distance between them, or she figured him for a hayseed who'd never seen the inside of anything bigger than a roadside motel. Either way, her lecture amused him. He'd seen the inside of more suites than she could shake her rear end at.

"Oh, my," she said in hushed tones as the elevator doors opened onto the penthouse floor. "Isn't this something?"

Geoff had to agree. A row of graceful Kentia palms lined each side of the white marble entry, leading the eye to the two huge Chinese porcelain vases that flanked the suite's carved mahogany double doors. In another time, it could have been the entrance to a sultan's royal chambers.

He opened the doors, ushering Randy into an octagonal foyer and smiling at her reaction. She murmured in delight, drawing her fingers along the marble top of a black lacquered bombé chest as she walked through to the living area, a spacious salon furnished with pastel upholstery and a junglelike profusion of exotic plants.

The walls were hung with prints of French impressionists, and the room's high ceilings were opened to the sapphire blue sky by skylights and clerestory windows. The living area flowed directly into the dining area, all of which was surrounded by an expansive terrace.

Geoff walked to the terrace doors and opened them to warm waves of heavily perfumed air and the jungle drumbeats of a samba street band. The Cariocas, as the natives of Rio were called, were already practicing feverishly for the parades to come. Pleasantly reminded of how Rio stimulated all of the senses, Geoff gazed out at the colored umbrellas that dotted Copacabana Beach across the way. The bay beyond was a glassy sheet of reflected sunlight that swept the attention

SURRENDER, BABY • 63

northeast, where Sugarloaf peak soared above the coastal mountains.

When he turned back, Randy was sitting at an antique writing desk, busily jotting down notes on a pad of paper. The woman needed to loosen up, he decided.

"Writing your memoirs?" Geoff asked. "What chapter am I?"

"You're the one entitled 'If He Has Long Hair and Rides a Motorcycle, Keep Your Eyes Open and Your Legs Closed.'" She flashed him an impertinent smile, then finished up whatever she was doing and rose from the desk to give him the paper.

Geoff skimmed a long list of dos and don'ts entitled "House Rules." The first item particularly intrigued him: "There will be no physical contact between the two parties involved during the course of the assignment," it said. The word *no* had been underlined three times. The next few items had to do with cohabitation etiquette, including a reference to unnecessary nudity and feet on the furniture.

"No feet on the furniture?" Geoff asked, feigning perplexity as he walked to the nearest couch, a delicate white loveseat with silky cushions. He flopped down and swung up his booted feet, resting them on the cushions. "Is this what you're talking about?" he asked, smiling quizzically. "I just want to be sure."

Caked dirt crumbled from his boot heels, soiling the pristine white silk. Randy drew in a sharp breath, then folded her arms as if to contain herself. Her dark eyebrows took on an attitude when she was angry, but it was the slight flare of her nostrils that really drove him crazy. Arousal tugged in the pit of his stomach. God, she was sexy. He loved crowding her. He loved watching her flare.

"You really are a bad-mannered brute, aren't you?" she said.

"Hey, I'm just trying to get your rules straight. What

was that other one? No unnecessary nudity?" He rose from the couch, flashing a slow grin as he stripped off his vest. It hadn't hit the floor before he'd caught hold of his T-shirt and pulled it over his head.

"What kind of nudity do you find unnecessary?" he asked, shaking out his hair as he let the shirt drop to the floor. "Is this nude enough for you? Or do I have to get bare-assed? I'm just trying to figure it out, sweetness."

A flush of heat crept up her throat. "Figure this out," she warned him. "If you take off one more stitch of clothing, I'll call hotel security and have you carted off to a jungle prison, where you'll rot and putrify like maggot food. And if you call me sweetness one more time, I'll—" She seemed to be struggling for something gruesome enough. "I'll poke out your eye with a sharp stick!"

"Now you've got me scared."

She glared threateningly, but Geoff only laughed, his hands on the tab fastener of his fatigue pants. She might be angry, but he could see by the way she was watching him that she wasn't unaffected by what she saw. Her focus seemed momentarily riveted on his upper torso, her breath quickening as she took in his golden body hair and the honed muscles of his chest and arms. As her gaze dropped to his pants, she shuddered.

"I don't have to put up with this," she said. "I can fire you."

She seemed to be fighting the desire to look down, which was just where he wanted her to look. He undid the tab, letting the waistband of his pants hang open. "Then who would find Hugh for you?"

"I'll find him myself. I don't need you."

"Don't be so sure." He moved as if to unzip his fly, and she gasped softly, her gaze darting to his crotch. Geoff felt a jolt of pleasure, almost as if she'd touched him there. His thoughts careened backward to another time when she *had* touched him there. He'd felt a fluttery lightness at first, like a hummingbird hovering near a flower, stealing some nectar, discovering and retreating, driving him wild.

"Why are you being like this?" she asked, interrupting his reverie just as it was getting good.

"Maybe because your rules don't make sense, Randy. They aren't realistic, especially the first one. Physical contact is hard to avoid when two people are living together in close quarters."

"These quarters aren't close."

"They could get close. Accidents happen." He waited a moment until she defiantly met his gaze, and then he started slowly toward her. She thrust a hand out to ward him off, but he paid no attention. He didn't stop, not completely, not until her hand was touching his bare chest.

The contact of skin on skin seemed to paralyze her. Her hand was rigid against his pectorals, but he could feel the erratic pulsebeat coursing through her fingertips. She was vibrating inside. Good. He wanted her as rattled as he was, as rattled as he'd been ten years ago.

"Close like now," he said. He glanced down at her hand, at her fingers nestling tautly in his chest hair, and felt a tightening all the way to the soles of his feet. Every part of his body was going hard on him, including the one she seemed so curious about. His heart began to pound and he wondered if she could feel its force. God knew he was feeling it. He was feeling things he couldn't remember ever experiencing before with another woman, except maybe her.

"Is this the physical contact you were talking about?" he asked. "Or was it something more like this?" He caught hold of her wrist, his grip firm as he drew her hand up, inching her closer to him.

"Stop it," she whispered.

"I almost wish I could. But I have a hard time doing that with you, Randy. A very hard time."

He tugged on her wrist, and she stumbled a little closer, cursing under her breath. But he didn't let up. He kept increasing the pressure until she was so close their thighs were brushing.

"I won't allow this," she hissed. "Either you let me go and agree never to touch me again, or—"

"Or what?"

"I want you out of here! Now!"

"Don't make idle threats, Randy. You'll never get to Santeras without me. You won't even be able to make contact. And if you did, you wouldn't last five minutes with a viper like him. He'd amuse himself with you until you were begging for mercy, and then he'd hand you over to his thugs."

He pulled her closer and bent toward her mouth. "You need me, Randy." His breath went husky and hot, bathing her face. "You need me, baby. Admit it."

She jerked her head away, refusing to submit, and at the same time, exposing the curve of her throat to him. He blew away strands of her silky dark hair, then drew his tongue lightly along the graceful arc of her neck, all the time locking her wrist so that she couldn't get away.

The urgent sound that slipped from her throat wasn't quite a moan . . . but it became one as he caught a tiny section of pale flesh between his teeth. He gave her a sharp little nip, then touched his lips to her reddening skin, a hummingbird kiss, light and hovering, just the way she'd tortured him on the bike.

"You need me, Randy."

She jerked back her hand. But when he wouldn't release her, she shuddered and softened. Slowly she turned her face back to his, and the liquid desire in her velvet eyes told him she was aroused, terribly aroused. She gazed up at him helplessly, her lips parted. "All right," she admitted, her voice a throb. "I need you . . . but don't do this. Don't take advantage."

She moved against him, her breath quickening. He didn't know what she was doing. She might have been trying to get away, but the silky float of her breasts against his bare chest was more invitation than he could resist.

His body urged him to do exactly what she was

asking him not to. *Go ahead, Dias,* a voice whispered. *Take advantage. Lay her down on that couch you just dirtied up and take whatever you can get. Take it all, just like she did.*

With his free hand he combed her hair, gathering it up like a ruffle of black silk as he gazed down at her. His body was pounding at him, talking to him, but he held off the voices, the inner forces. There was gratification in knowing he could control the impulses, in knowing he could curb desire. It was all part of the self-mastery he sought.

Just a kiss, he told himself. One stolen kiss.

He covered her mouth with his, moving against her, shocked at the hunger he felt. His hands curled into fists, lifting her, pressing her body into his as if he could make up for all the years of waiting with this one kiss. She resisted for an instant, her lips taut against his, but then, as he took hold of her face and began to gentle her, his fingers stroking her jaw, his thumb playing at the sensitive corner of her mouth, she seemed to melt.

"Don't make me do this," she pleaded, but the throaty quality of her voice sounded more like urgent need than a refusal.

"Kiss me back, Randy," he said.

She shuddered, but her answering moan told him all the fight had gone out of her. She was yielding to whatever forces had built inside her. He released her wrist, and his hands fell immediately to her waist, then slid to her hips, her buttocks. Her trembling increased as he cupped her, and she raised her arms in a gesture of such helplessness it made him suddenly, painfully harder. His fingers curled hungrily into her soft flesh.

The urge for completion was like a force of nature inside him. He hardly knew how to stave it off. And yet, at the same time, he realized he had no intention of taking advantage in the way she meant, not then, not yet. He'd seen the heat in her eyes when she looked at him, the erotic fascination. That might have been enough incentive for him once, but he wanted more than simple physical lust from her now. He wanted the satisfaction of hearing her utter his name with the same passionate conviction with which she said Hugh's. He wanted to be the man she dreamed of.

His breath shook with the effort it took to control himself. He touched her lips lightly, wanting to deepen the kiss, to take possession of her with his mouth. Muscles were tightening at the base of his body, aching. But somewhere in the midst of all his pent-up ardor, he heard a strange faint sound.

At first it was just a soft shrill in the depths of his consciousness. He hardly heard it, and even when he did, he dismissed it as some errant impulse from his nervous system, just blood roaring in his ears. But it became louder and more insistent, and finally he realized it was something else, a telephone or a door.

Bells were ringing. And someone was shouting in a Portuguese accent. It took him another moment to connect the bell and the shouting. It was their bags, he realized. The porter was at the door with their bags.

"What is that?" Randy asked, gazing up at him as though she'd just emerged from another plane of consciousness.

"I think you've been saved by the bellboy," Geoff said. She drew back, but continued to cling to him, her hands on his shoulders as if she wasn't sure she'd be able to stand on her own. She seemed even more vulnerable in that moment than when he'd been kissing her, and it made him want to sweep her up and carry her to a bedroom.

"Go ahead," she said, stepping back and waving him toward the door. "Answer it. I'm all right."

"I wish that made two of us," he said under his breath. He was glad for the looseness of his fatigue pants as he headed for the door.

The porter turned out to be a rail-thin young boy who was frantic to please as he rolled the luggage cart into the room. He rushed to unload the luggage, struggling

with one of Randy's heavy suitcases first. Geoff immediately took pity and helped him. When they'd finished,
he pulled a ten-dollar bill from the money clip in his
pocket and ushered the boy to the door. "Don't call us,
we'll call you," he said, tucking the money into the shirt
pocket of the kid's uniform.

As he turned back to Randy, he saw that she was
staring out the windows, her arms tightly folded. She
was still trembling, and Geoff didn't need to be told
why. He knew exactly what was troubling her. She was
thinking about how close they'd come to making love
and what would have happened if they had. Despite all
of her pleas and his quest for control, they would have
been all over each other, crazy, hungry, just like ten
years ago. He knew that as well as he knew his name,
rank, and serial number. And she knew it too.

"Ouch," Randy said softly as she plucked a stubborn
hair from the inner arch of her eyebrow. It was past
midnight, her bedroom door was barricaded against
the enemy, and the ritual of purification had begun.
She sat on her bed, cross-legged, a cosmetic mirror in
one hand, tweezers in the other.

Whenever she was frustrated or anxious she plunged
herself into some insignificant but intensely concentrated activity. Counting backward was just one of the
devices she used. If she was at home, she cross-indexed
her personal library or bleached the grout in her bathroom tiles, scrubbing the grooves with a stiff tooth-
brush until they were snowy white. If she was at the
office, she reorganized her Rolodex or reprogrammed
her high-tech message phone. Often the focused action
alone could restore her sense of control.

She was neither place tonight, so personal grooming
would have to suffice. She'd just given herself a mani-
cure and a pedicure, and now she was restructuring
the shape of her eyebrows, admittedly a dangerous

thing to do when one was distraught. She could easily end up looking like an extra from "Star Trek," a Vulcan science officer.

She angled the mirror to catch the light from the table lamp beside the bed, then tweaked a tiny offending dark hair from the space between her brows. Tears stung her eyes, and she swore softly, setting the tweezers down. Not surprisingly, the ritual wasn't working. It would take more than four coats of Wild Coral Kiss nail polish and Greta Garbo eyebrows to prepare her for the next go-around with Geoff Dias.

The man had a devastating effect on her. His strange green eyes were hypnotic, and his seemingly inhuman control made her feel defenseless against him. It didn't seem to matter that she held womanizers like him in total contempt. It didn't even seem to matter that she was engaged to be married. When he touched her, she was entrapped, helpless.

She tested her toenails for dryness, then plucked the cotton balls from between her toes. "You would have loved him, Edna," she murmured, speaking as if her deceased mother were there. "He's beautiful, he's sexier than sin—and he's a black-hearted devil if I ever saw one. He even rides a motorcycle with a broken heart on it."

Sliding off the bed, she headed for the lavishly appointed marble-and-brass bathroom. "He doesn't seem to care a damn that he might be ruining my life," she added, continuing her soliloquy as she disposed of the cotton balls in the wastebasket. "All he wants is to salve his male ego because I disappeared on him. Being dumped must have been a brand-new experience for him, poor baby. He's probably used to women worshiping at his feet."

As Randy came out of her troubled reflections, she caught her own image in the wall of mirrors and hesitated, scrutinizing her pensive expression. There were purple smudges under her dark eyes, and her normal healthy flush had faded to paleness. She should have been in bed asleep—or if nothing else, thinking about how to find her fiancé. Instead, she was obsessively sifting through the lurid details of her most recent encounter with Geoff Dias.

"All he wants is to prove that he can have me," she said, fingering the silk bodice of her black lace-trimmed teddy. The shivery sensations he evoked stirred inside her as she realized she was absently caressing herself with the cool, slick material. "Once he's accomplished that, he'll discard me, just like all those men discarded Edna."

Staring in the mirror, thinking about the effect he had on her, she watched her eyes melt with dark pleasure and the flush return to her face. She tilted her chin, looking for the tender spot where he'd nipped her throat, and the strangest sensation of excitement spiraled in the depths of her belly. It wasn't bad enough that he aroused her. She had to do it to herself!

She switched off the bathroom lights as she went out, then fell across the bed diagonally, pulling a pillow into her arms and resting her head on it. She tried to shut off her thoughts, but she couldn't shut off her bodily responses. She felt as trembly as the moonlight shimmering across the bay, as loose and flowing as the water. Even when she drew up her legs, it did nothing to stop the excitement swirling inside her.

There was a part of her that wanted to go with the feelings. She couldn't deny it. There had been moments in the years since she'd been with him that she'd caught herself remembering, almost reveling in the memories of what they'd done. And then the shame had hit her, the guilt and the fear. Fear that she had fallen heir to Edna's curse, that she would start to like the way Geoff Dias made her feel, start to need it . . .

She couldn't let that happen. There was too much at stake. "E . . . N . . . O," she whispered, beginning to count backward.

Six

Geoff held the tumbler of rum to his breastbone and rolled it back and forth across his chest, absorbing the cold shock of the ice-filled glass against the heat of his body. He half expected to see steam rise off his skin. He'd lost track of the time, but it had to be at least two in the morning, and the temperature hadn't dropped all that much from the high nineties of the late afternoon when they'd arrived. It was going to be one long, sultry bitch of a night.

Pulsing waves of Latin music rolled up to him from the street several stories below his bedroom balcony. A mounting frenzy seemed to have taken over the city in anticipation of Carnaval. Street bands beat out jungle rhythms on their drums, and throngs of tawny-skinned Cariocas danced and cavorted in the same bikinis they'd worn to the beach. They were practicing for the parades that would start in less than twenty-four hours, and nothing could wilt their spirits, not even the heat and steambath humidity.

He leaned against the balcony railing, holding the drink in both hands, his weight on his forearms as he watched the undulating dancers. Once it had started, Carnaval would run nonstop until Ash Wednesday, four days of wildly hedonistic and blatantly sensual celebration. Most Cariocas threw themselves into the revelry with total abandon. They donned elaborate costumes for the *desfiles*, as the parades were called. Men became women, or demons, or magical animals. Women became samba snakes, high priestesses of sensuality, both slave and mistress to the throbbing, unrelenting dance music.

Sex on parade, Geoff thought, remembering the Carnavals of his past. He'd celebrated the event, also known as Mardi Gras, all over the world, in Rio, France, New Orleans. It was always the same—a full-tilt striptease of the senses, where everyday conventions were wantonly discarded and normal behavior was totally unacceptable.

Geoff could think of only one other experience in his life that came anywhere close to the sexual spontaneity and dark excitement of Carnaval. And that experience was far more memorable in its way. . . .

He'd thought he was having a dream the night he caught sight of a virginal vision in a wedding gown walking down the lonely stretch of highway. She was carrying her high heels and an open bottle of champagne. When he pulled up alongside her on his bike, she threatened to break the bottle over his head if he came near her.

He'd finally convinced her she wasn't safe out alone that time of night, and she'd reluctantly climbed on behind him, but not before telling him in no uncertain terms what no-good bastards men were. She'd railed about how her mother had always picked men who broke her heart—users, losers, and dance-away lovers. How she herself, determined not to repeat her mother's mistakes, had fallen in love with the perfect man, a brilliant and wealthy young medical researcher, only to have him jilt her because his parents didn't approve of her.

The tirade left her weepy and trembling. But once she

was finished, she wiped the tears from her dark eyes and tilted her chin at the world. "Everybody thinks I'm a bad girl anyway," she'd said defiantly, arranging her full skirt on the bike behind him and curling her arms tightly around his waist. "So I might as well be one."

Geoff figured he'd latched onto a beautiful lunatic. His plan was to get her to the nearest phone booth, call a taxi, and send her home. That was before he realized she had something else in mind. It seemed as if one minute she was clutching him and sobbing against his back, and the next, she was touching him. It couldn't have happened that fast, but everything must have accelerated in his mind when he glanced down and saw where her hands were.

She was very tentative at first, as if he were a bomb she was trying to defuse blindfolded. But her trembling fingers didn't stay tentative. She turned him into a wild man. Before she was through with him, she had him so hot, he drove the bike into an alley, pulled her onto his lap, and took her right there in her wedding dress.

They climaxed like exploding stars, but it wasn't enough. They found a motel room and made love all night. It wasn't until after they'd spent themselves that she began to cry again. He wanted to hold her, but she wouldn't let him. She was horrified at what she'd done and even more embittered about men and love. That's when he'd begun to realize how out of character their night of wildness was for her. She didn't have to tell him. Her anguish spoke for her. She'd never done anything like that before—and never would again. . . .

With a hard sigh, Geoff pushed back from the railing and drained the tumbler of rum. Dampness broke out on his temples as the liquor seared his throat. He'd been fairly jaded up to that point in his life. He'd thought there was nothing new under the sun where women were concerned, but he'd never known the intensity, the raw, sweet turbulence of Randy's passion.

Like Carnaval, she'd broken all the rules of normal behavior. She'd turned his world on its axis, reversed his expectations. He still hadn't recovered from the shock of it. And nothing shocked Geoff Dias.

He turned and walked into his bedroom, knowing her room was just across the way. Staring at the door, he was aware of the mounting tension in his thigh muscles, the spillway of energy into his groin. He would have loved nothing better than to turn the tables, to catch her off guard while she was sleeping and make her as blind with need as she'd made him.

Instead he went to the desk, set down the empty tumbler, and pulled a piece of hotel stationery from the drawer. *Time to exorcise some demons*, he told himself.

Randy woke to the moist languor of mid-morning, the slow whir of ceiling fans and the soft screech of a jungle bird. As the sounds penetrated her consciousness, she remembered where she was: Rio de Janeiro . . . the River of January, with its exotic rain forests, miles of white crescent beaches, and steamy tropical nights.

Images of Rio were filtering through her awareness like a travel brochure as she opened her eyes and realized she was exactly where she'd fallen asleep, curled up around the pillow, still wearing her teddy. She'd never put on a nightgown or turned down the bed covers.

Sheened in perspiration, slowed by the weight of the moist heat that enveloped her, she untangled herself from the pillow and pushed up to a sitting position. Someone had opened the French doors to the balcony off her bedroom, she realized. She glanced in confusion at the door to her room, which was still locked. A hotel maid? How did she get in?

A brilliant orange and turquoise macaw was perched on the balcony's white wrought-iron railings, gazing at her with unblinking eyes. As she stared back at the magnificent bird, uncertain that it was real, a garland of yellow butterflies flitted by. The travel brochures were right, she thought. This was paradise. Pots of exotic orchids dotted the balcony, and the breezes that wafted into the room were so heavy with their perfume, they seemed tinted a blush pink like the flowers.

She rolled her neck slowly, feeling logy and stiff, as if she'd been doing something she shouldn't have the night before. It must have been the macaw's cry that woke her up, but otherwise she seemed to be alone. As she slid around to get off the bed, she noticed something lying on the bed's other pillow . . . a pen and ink sketch.

She was almost afraid to pick it up. From her vantage point it looked suspiciously like a drawing of a man and a woman in some kind of erotic ecstasy, and she knew who the artist must be. Her heart began to pound as she angled nearer, trying to see what it was without actually touching it, as if she could somehow make the images less disturbing that way. Finally she gave in to her feverish curiosity and picked the paper up.

Her mouth went dry as she stared at the drawing. He'd captured the raw, forbidden intimacy of their night together with a few graceful, slashing strokes of his pen. She was fully clothed in the picture, but the sweetheart sleeves of her wedding dress had dropped off her shoulders, baring one of her breasts for all the world to see. Worse, she was sitting on Geoff's lap, facing him, straddling him, just as she had on the bike. Her head was thrown back, her spine arched in swooning ecstasy as he slid his hand up her skirt.

It wasn't clear whether they were intimately joined, but it was crystal clear that she was a consenting adult to whatever they were doing. More than consenting, she looked like a woman in the throes of rapture—eager, wanton, drugged with passion. And he looked like a man totally confident of his sexual power over her.

The sketch brought back vivid memories, and such

sharp sensations of physical pleasure that Randy could hardly catch her breath. She hated admitting even to herself that he'd brought her to such a fever pitch of desire. And it humiliated her to remember how shamelessly she'd behaved with him.

How dare he draw what they'd done? He was invading her privacy, exposing her. She knew she was being foolish. It made no sense allowing herself to feel hurt or betrayed by a man who probably practiced seduction with the same dedication that a preacher practiced religion. But she did feel hurt. She couldn't help herself.

She told herself to throw the picture away, but for some reason she couldn't do it. Her wrist locked and her fingers began to shake as she gathered the paper together to crush it. Instead, she slammed the stationery face down and covered it with the pillow, as if she could make it disappear or smother the writhing carnal energy out of it.

She left the bed and walked to the French doors, aware of the sunshine pouring over her like honey from a pitcher as she stepped out onto the balcony. She should have felt warm, but she didn't. There were too many conflicting emotions tangled up inside her. She had no idea how to deal with the problem of Geoff Dias, but she had to find a way. This couldn't go on any longer. She had to confront him. Harder still, she had to confront her feelings for him.

Once she'd showered and dressed, she found him on the penthouse terrace having breakfast. He'd changed from fatigue pants to faded khaki shorts and a ribbed cotton tank top, and his legs were long and tanned and dusted with golden hair. The table he sat at was facing the horizon, a stunning, seamless backdrop of dense blue sky and equally blue water.

He was staring out to sea, and Randy was hesitant to disturb his meditation. He looked absorbed in his thoughts, almost peaceful. Sunlight filtered through the *palmeira* that shaded him, catching errant tendrils of his hair as the breezes lifted them. It gilded the long strands like spun gold, making him seem almost ethereal, a god at rest, the artist in a moment of contemplation.

The table next to him was set with a sterling silver coffee service and a platter of crusty rolls and sticky, pecan-studded buns. Another large platter held rainbow tiers of the fruits of the country, including wedges of melon, mango, deep-red papaya, and a heap of luscious Brazilian figs.

The air was balmy warm and the scene so bucolic, Randy felt almost mollified, as if Mother Nature herself was cautioning her, "Don't worry, be happy." No wonder people loved the tropics, she thought. The weather lulled you into abandoning your concerns—along with your inhibitions. However, as much as she wanted to sit down, eat a mango, and relax, she had to talk with him. She had to lay down the law.

He glanced up at her as she approached, a sidelong look that said he'd been expecting her. His green eyes shimmered with anticipation.

She held the picture up for him to see, but kept it just out of his reach, as if too close a look might titillate him. She didn't want to remind him of what he'd drawn—or what they'd done. "I consider this a gross violation of my privacy," she said with no preamble whatsoever.

"Sit down," he invited, motioning to the wrought-iron chair across from him. "Have some coffee. It's Brazilian, strong enough to pour itself."

She remained standing, unyielding. "How did you get in my room?"

In no particular hurry, he took a drink of his *cafezinho*, a tiny cup of sweetened black coffee, then tore off a yeasty section of sweet roll and ate it. "Locked doors are my business," he said finally.

"Then tonight I'll barricade it."

"Don't waste your time, Randy. You could lock yourself in a bank vault, and it wouldn't stop me, not if I wanted to get in."

"Really?" Her voice was inching toward shrillness. "I never knew you were so talented. An artist, a safe-cracker—what else?"

His quick smile held a sexy warning. *You haven't seen anything yet*, it said. He checked out her outfit, hesitating on the halter top of her sundress as if he were waiting for her to swoon, arch her back, and pop out a breast so he could draw another picture.

Impulsively, Randy held out the sketch, crushed it in her fist, and dropped the wad of paper on the table.

His smile faded, which pleased her immensely.

"We have to talk." She pulled a chair out from the table and seated herself, her heart creating a terrible uproar. Her rigid stance warned him not to push her any further. But what would she do if he did? Every confrontation with him was freighted with risk. She could spar with him verbally, but she was no match for him in any other way.

He simply settled back, folded his arms, and gazed at her. "By all means. Talk. Amaze me some more."

She felt a stab of pain near her ear and realized she must be clenching her jaw. She was sure to have a headache before this was over with. "If you'll remember, I made up a list of house rules—"

"I do remember. They specified no physical contact, but they didn't say anything about drawing pictures."

"Would it have made any difference if they had?"

"Probably not."

"Geoff, this has got to stop—"

"I like that," he said softly. "I like it when you say my name. I don't think I've ever heard you say it before."

He sounded grainy voiced and slightly surprised. The curiosity in his expression made him seem sincere. Randy felt a softening inside, a loosening of tight muscles and tighter inhibitions. She fought to control the reaction, aware that it was easier dealing with him when he was being perverse. When he was civil, or God forbid, nice, she didn't know how to defend herself.

"You may not hear me say it again," she told him, determined to be tough. "If you don't agree to my rules, it's over. The deal's off. I'll find Hugh without you."

"Never going to happen," he warned.

"You won't agree to the rules?"

"No—you'll never find Hugh."

"And you'll never get what you want."

"Which is?"

She hesitated, nearly light-headed from the way her pulse was racing. "A night. One night . . . with me."

The slow lift of his chin betrayed his surprise. "A repeat performance?" he said. "You and me?"

"Yes." She'd played the wild card, her only bargaining chip with him. She hated having to resort to such a desperate tactic, feeling as if she were going against everything she believed in about honesty, and personal ethics—but she had no other options left. If Geoff thought they were going to make love at a later point, perhaps he would leave her alone for now, and they could both concentrate on finding Hugh. She was counting on that being the case, and she needed the time it would buy her. When they found Hugh . . . well, she would deal with that problem when the time came.

He tapped the porcelain coffee cup with his forefinger. "Since you put it that way," he said, glancing up at her through lowered lashes.

"You agree, then?"

He shrugged, a gesture of surrender. "Do with me what you will. I'm yours to command."

"Good. As long as you understand that I'm calling the shots, then let's get started."

"Doing what?"

"Looking for Hugh, of course. I want to begin our investigation."

"*Our* investigation?"

"Yes, I want to be involved. I think we should start with the American consulate, then the local police."

He was shaking his head slowly. "I'd suggest we avoid the red tape of the official investigation and go straight to the source. I speak enough Portuguese and French to be understood by the locals. With some luck, we can trace Hugh's steps directly, starting with the hotel he was staying at."

"All right," she said hesitantly. She was more than prepared to make concessions if it meant speeding things up. It only made sense to let him handle the investigation. He was the expert at finding people, but at least now she had veto power.

Relaxing a little, she poured herself a cup of the rich black coffee and took one of the crusty rolls, aware that he was watching her with undisguised interest. He was probably wondering what kind of woman would do the things she'd done—get involved with a stranger on the road and then, ten years later, strike a sexual bargain with that same stranger. Most men would have concluded that she was either desperate or a woman of easy virtue. She imagined Geoff Dias thought she was both . . . and she was beginning to wonder if he was right.

She poured enough milk in the coffee to make it drinkable, then sipped it slowly, aware that it was too potent a brew to simply relax and enjoy, and yet at the same time, that it was undoubtedly habit-forming . . . not unlike him.

Finally she set the cup down and turned to him, ready to unburden herself. She was surprised to see that he had smoothed out the drawing she'd crumpled. He was studying it with an expression that she couldn't immediately put a name to. Reflective, perhaps. Moody. Yes, he looked rather distracted.

"You have to understand that Hugh is the man I love," she told him. "I'm engaged to marry him, and I'd make any sacrifice to get him back, even . . . "

"Sleeping with me?" he finished as she hesitated.

"Even that."

"The ultimate torture?"

When she didn't answer, he rose from the chair and walked to the wrought-iron railing that bordered the terrace. Turning his back to the bright blue sky, he leaned against the railing and stared at her. Haloed by sunlight, his face and body carved by shadows, he was breathtaking. The green of his eyes was brilliant, as though lit by an emotion even the shade couldn't subdue.

Arrested by the juxtaposition of man and nature, by the simplicity of his casual pose, Randy admitted to herself that she was far more attracted to him than she ever had been to Hugh. Irresistibly physically attracted.

And yet she knew physical attraction to a man wasn't enough. It could ruin a woman. It had ruined her mother's life. A man had to have character. He had to be stable and dependable. But try as she would to convince herself that she shouldn't be affected by Geoff Dias, the shakiness in her stomach wouldn't go away. She felt as loose and fluttery as the butterflies wafting overhead. It seemed she was like her mother, doomed to be drawn to the wrong kind of man.

"I want to be with Hugh," she said, uttering the words softly, urgently.

"You may want to be with him, but you don't love him. If I believed you did, I wouldn't be here."

His voice was husky again, compellingly sincere. It made her feel strange and vulnerable when he talked that way. It made her throat ache. "Why are you doing this to me?" she asked. "What do you want?"

"Why did you do it to me? What was the point of seducing me and running off?"

Randy thought she saw a flaring of pain in his eyes, but it was gone so quickly, she couldn't be sure. She would never be sure with him, she realized. That was the problem. "I don't know why I did it. I was hurting and terribly angry. Everybody thought I was a wild kid anyway, probably because of Edna. Since I already had the reputation, I thought I might as well live up to it."

"So I was an experiment, an opportunity to find out just how wild you could be with a renegade biker?"

"Yes, maybe—I don't know. I wasn't thinking in those terms. I wasn't thinking at all, I guess."

"Nothing's changed, has it?" he said, almost bitterly. "Did it ever occur to you that I was anything more than an extension of that motorcycle, Randy? That I might have some feelings about what happened between us?"

She searched his face, looking for any evidence of the feelings he mentioned. He was good at hiding them. He was one of the coolest characters she'd ever come across, almost as if he were determined to control every vulnerable response, down to the tiniest spasm of nerves. And yet there was a darkness glowing in his features, a brightness glittering in the depths of his eyes that couldn't be controlled. They fascinated her, those glimpses of his inner world. She wanted to know what Geoff Dias was protecting, what he was feeling.

"I wasn't trying to hurt anyone," she told him. "But apparently I did, both of us. I'm sorry."

She hesitated, waiting for a response. When he didn't react, she probed a little further. "You seem so determined to prove that Hugh is wrong for me," she said. "Why do you care? Did what happen between us shake you up that badly?"

He flared without warning, striding toward her, pulling her out of the chair. "I'll tell you when I'm hurting, sweetness. You'll be the first to know." His voice was low, almost harsh as he noticed the hand he was gripping, the bright coral polish she'd painted on her nails.

"What's the occasion?" he asked. "Is this for me?"

Randy was too shaken to remind him of the house rules. "Not for you," she said angrily, "*because* of you. I needed a distraction, but don't flatter yourself that it means anything."

His hand tightened on her wrist as he glared at her, caught somewhere between male rage and the need to control it. Seconds ticked by, each one a tiny bomb exploding in Randy's head. She was no match for him. She couldn't possibly stop him if he decided to get physical, if he decided to—

"Let's get going," he said abruptly. "The sooner we find your beloved fiancé, the sooner you pay up."

His fingers were biting into her flesh, but there was something in his voice, a tone, a drumbeat, that told Randy he was more than angry. He was dangerously jealous.

Seven

"A motorcycle?" Randy hesitated, casting a suspicious glance at the gleaming black low-rider conspicuously parked in the crescent-shaped driveway that fronted their hotel. "Where did that come from?" Now she understood why Geoff hadn't called a taxi as she'd suggested. She'd thought he was still angry.

Geoff brushed past her and walked to the sleek machine. "Must be black magic," he said sardonically. "We need transportation and a bike materializes." He settled himself on the leather seat like a cowboy sliding into a new saddle he was looking forward to breaking in. "Actually, I had the hotel concierge rent it for me," he said by way of explanation as he gripped the handlebars and generally got the feel of the bike.

"Don't they rent *cars* in this country?" Randy asked.

Geoff glanced up and caught her off guard. His eyes were as cold and green as a slick ocean surface. Randy could feel the chill. She sensed the undercurrents. He *was* still angry.

"You coming?" It was more a command than a question.

With bells on, she thought, but didn't say it.

Moments later they were rolling down Avenida Atlantica, the famous ocean boulevard that paralleled Copacabana Beach. The heavy traffic forced them to go slowly, allowing Randy to relax a little and soak up the ambience. Everywhere she looked, strolling troubadours were playing mandolins and young boys were beating feverishly on bongo drums.

The rich smells of buttered popcorn and caramel wafted from pushcarts as beach vendors energetically hawked their wares. A wizened older man labored to carry a huge red umbrella studded with woven straw sunhats for sale, while a young girl held up a rainbowlike array of cotton candy, that looked like mountains of clouds.

Randy found herself so distracted by the colorful commotion, she almost forgot she was hostage to a bad-tempered mercenary and his rumbling, grumbling motorcycle. Dizzying mosaic patterns decorated the sidewalks that fronted the beach, and the expanse of white sand beyond was swarming with sunbathers of all sizes, ages, and colors. If Cariocas worshiped the sun, they also worshiped the human body, Randy realized. The common goal seemed to be to expose as much skin as possible to the elements.

Fascinated by the spectacle, she watched near-naked children frolic in the surf and small groups of topless women stroll unselfconsciously over the sand, their breasts bobbing as they walked, their lithe bodies glistening in the sun. Every now and then she caught a whiff of rich suntan lotion mingled with the pungency of moist, hot female flesh.

Geoff was undoubtedly distracted too, she imagined.

The traffic slowed in front of them, and as Geoff geared down, Randy became reacquainted with the powerful vibrations of the machine beneath her. They trembled through her clenched thighs and radiated up her body almost pleasurably. Normally she would have felt compelled to cut off the sensations, but today she found herself contemplating her responses, tuning in to them as she wondered what it would be like to experience such feelings willingly, and without fear.

She was also aware of the potent tropical sunshine pouring its heat over the city, and of the throbbing native drums that saturated the air with their fervent sensuality. Closing her eyes for a moment, she allowed the drumbeats to fill her senses and the motorcycle's deep vibrations to course through her body. As the energy zinged out to her fingertips and down to her toes, she found herself smiling, beginning to understand the thrill of a big bike. It had to be terribly exhilarating having all that horsepower at your command.

She clutched Geoff tighter as he veered to avoid the blockage in the traffic ahead. He roared down the open lane, only to slow down again as they pulled up to an intersection. As they waited for the light to change, a beautiful, dusky-skinned Carioca woman in a *tanga*, a micro-string bikini, drifted past them on her way to the beach.

Fio dental, Randy thought, remembering the Portuguese phrase she'd heard used for such bikinis. Dental floss. The woman was small-breasted, lissome, and perfectly proportioned for such a naked display of femininity. She was also supremely confident of her appeal.

Inexplicably Randy felt a stab of something that must have been envy. She couldn't see Geoff's expression, but she knew he must be watching the exotic woman, and she was curious about what was going through his mind. Sex, of course. But sex with whom?

There were plenty of muscular, half-naked men meandering around in thongs and bikini briefs, but when Randy looked at them, she found herself thinking of Geoff, of how he would look in a bathing suit. She was visited by vivid images of his long bronzed legs, of hardened muscles swirled with golden hair, of firm buttocks, and the way those tiny briefs lovingly cupped a man's private parts. Much like a woman's hand, she realized.

Much like her hand?

The thought was electrifying. Randy couldn't catch her breath for the force of it. She felt light-headed, but the sensations in the pit of her stomach were anything but. They were deep, shivery, and sharp. This was what happened when you surrendered to physical stimulation, she told herself. You got stimulated, genius!

As they continued toward their destination, Randy set about to distract herself with relaxation techniques, but try as she might, she couldn't get that last image out of her head. When Geoff pulled the motorcycle up in front of the luxury hotel Hugh had stayed at, she was still thinking about men's bodies and women's hands.

"What are you looking at?" Geoff asked as he swung off the bike and caught her staring.

Randy forced her gaze above his beltline. "Was I . . . looking? Sorry, I must be preoccupied."

"Preoccupied with my pants?"

"No! I was thinking about, well—swimming, if you must know." Not exactly a brilliant parry, but he'd caught her off guard.

He cocked his head as if waiting for the punchline.

"I happen to be a very good swimmer," she informed him, unable to completely resist his golden smile. "I spent a summer as a lifeguard trainee at the beach, and I pulled more than one drowning boogie boarder out of the surf."

"Lucky dogs. Maybe you could save my life some-time?"

"That all depends." Randy was aware that their interaction had taken on a certain bantering rhythm, a man-woman thing she and Hugh rarely indulged in. "Is yours a life worth saving?"

"Well, now, if I'm being called upon to justify my existence, that's going to take some time. Give me several hours of your undivided attention and I'll try to prove myself worthy."

"Several hours? You must have a lot to prove."

"You're a lot of woman, sweetness. If I remember correctly, you can be pretty exacting."

Randy flushed, remembering too. She'd had her moments that night, boldly telling him what she liked and didn't like. He must have thought he was dealing with a woman of the world, when quite the opposite was true. She'd been an eighteen-year-old virgin, desperate to forget that she'd been jilted, woozy from champagne, and probably drunk with power over the way she'd aroused a seemingly dangerous man like Geoff. Geoff couldn't possibly have known she'd never been to bed with a man before that night; there had been no telltale pain or blood.

She'd wondered about that afterward. She knew girls often lost the protective membrane during the normal physical activity of childhood. Nevertheless, it had worried her. Maybe she had believed that some pain or physical difficulty would have been a fitting atonement for her sins that night. The lack of it had made everything seem too easy. It had made her seem easy, too, like Edna. And nothing frightened her more than the possibility of sharing her mother's fate. Perhaps that was why she hadn't allowed herself to be sexually intimate since, not even with Hugh.

"You want to get off?" Geoff asked.

The question startled Randy out of her thoughts. "I beg your *pardon*?"

His shoulders jerked with husky laughter. "Off the bike, you ninny."

"Oh!" Randy flushed with surprise, then began to laugh despite herself. She shook her head, hopelessly embarrassed about what she'd thought he meant. She really *was* preoccupied.

He held out a hand, apparently to assist her.

Still flustered, she let him steady her as she swung

her leg over the bike and slid off. What she hadn't counted on were the mosaic patterns woven into the sidewalk. They undulated like ocean waves, moving crazily as she tried to focus her eyes on them. Dizziness swamped her, and she gripped Geoff's hand tightly, trying to catch her balance. The next thing she knew she was lurching straight at him.

He blocked her fall with his body, gathering her up in his arms. "You okay?"

"Give me a minute," she said, clinging to him dizzily. He held her close, but Randy couldn't ignore the fact that he was shaking with silent laughter. "I could have sworn you tugged me," she accused.

"Hey, I just saved you from a bump on the head," he pointed out, holding her back and gazing at her with apparent sincerity as he straightened the strap of her sundress. "That must be worth something."

"Very kind of you." She wanted to be sardonic, but instead she actually smiled and blushed as if she were back in junior high, flirting with a boy in front of her locker. It was rather pleasant being in his arms, she had to admit, and he did smell wonderful, sort of like oranges and wild strawberries. Maybe it was that stuff he carried in his flask.

"However," she was careful to clarify, "when I referred to your worth earlier, I was thinking more along the lines of your moral character."

"Moral, immoral, what's the difference when you're in love?"

"When you're . . . what?" Her pulse began to race uncontrollably. "What do you mean?" she asked, her face going hot with curiosity. She could see the amusement shimmering in his green eyes. Of course he hadn't meant it, not the way she was thinking. Had he? It was clear he wasn't going to answer her question, and she suddenly felt angry at how breathless she'd become . . . at how much she'd apparently wanted him to mean something he hadn't meant.

"Who started this conversation anyway?" she asked, backing out of his arms and straightening her dress.

"I think you did, fair lady. Right after I caught you eyeballing my crotch."

"Did *not!*"

"Did so."

"Dream on, Dias."

"I don't have to dream, Witherspoon. You've been unzipping my fly with your eyes since the day I walked into your office. Ask nice and I might let you do the honors."

She should have been angry, but she found herself wanting to shake her head and laugh again. It was too absurd. And too true. She couldn't seem to tear her gaze away from his lower torso. Like it or not, she'd apparently picked up the family talent for crotch watching. The way she was going, it would soon be her badge of distinction. Edna would have been proud.

"What's that secret smile all about?" he questioned.

"For me to know, Dias." She brushed past him, feigning an air of breezy confidence and headed for the hotel's entrance.

Geoff watched her go, his gaze drawn automatically to the purposeful snap and sway of her hips. She was a pistol, he acknowledged, as hot as gunpowder. Success hadn't changed Randy Witherspoon any. She could call herself Miranda, she could wear designer clothes and satin teddies, but no amount of buffing would ever take the street kid out of her. She still led with her chin.

Aware of the pleasurable tightness in his gut, he smiled. Her go-to-hell attitude had served her well. It had probably got her where she was today. Too bad it was about to get her into big trouble.

He turned back to the bike, fished a Hawaiian shirt of green and turquoise silk from the saddlebag, and drew it on over his tank top and shorts. He would find her Prince Charming for her. He had a hunch Hugh Hargrove was still in Rio somewhere, and that meant he could be located. But Geoff was in no particular hurry. He was far more interested in having Randy come face to face with the truth. She needed him for more than detective work, and he wanted her to know it. He wanted the satisfaction of hearing her say it. Oh, yes, that was exactly what he wanted from Randy Witherspoon. *Satisfaction.*

By that afternoon Geoff had a small measure of the reckoning he sought. He'd hung back, letting Randy take the lead in their investigation, until finally all of her attempts to get information about Hugh had been frustrated. The Swiss hotel manager would say nothing beyond confirming that Hugh had been a guest. When Randy had pressed him, he referred her to the local police, insisting he'd told them everything he knew.

She'd tried the hotel housekeeping staff next, but none of them had spoken enough English to be understood, and they'd all denied having seen Hugh when she produced his picture. It was clear to Geoff that she was being stonewalled. No one wanted to get involved in police matters and missing-persons investigations unless it was worth their while. At last, in frustration, she'd attempted to bribe the haughty maitre d' of the hotel restaurant. She'd had the right idea, Geoff conceded, but the wrong guy. In a flurry of indignation, the maitre d' escorted them out of the hotel.

"What do we do now?" she asked as they stood by the curb where the bike was parked. Even in the blast-furnace heat of late afternoon, samba music could be heard in the distance, probably coming from car radios turned up full notch.

Her question alone was an admission of defeat, Geoff realized. But he wasn't letting her off the hook that easily. "Maybe you could try the doorman," he suggested, using her own words. "Show a little thigh, promise some action? It worked for me the day I showed up at your office."

"Right," she intoned sarcastically. "It worked so well, you left me standing in an alley with one stocking. Come on, Dias. I need some help here."

Her frustration was obvious, but he couldn't make up his mind whether she'd been humbled enough. The fire in her dark eyes was still smoldering, and the way her nostrils did that cute little flaring thing made him hot.

"*Pleeeze*," she said wearily, angrily.

"You're catching on." He straightened the strap of her sundress and smiled. "Ask nice and ye shall receive."

Twenty minutes and several taxi drivers later, Geoff had their first solid lead. One of the drivers that serviced the hotel recognized Hugh's picture. The man was more than cooperative when Geoff slipped him a bill of a very large denomination. He offered to take Geoff directly to the nightclub where he'd driven Hugh. "Many times," he added in Portuguese. "Many nights I drive him there."

Geoff asked a few more pertinent questions, then found Randy wilted in a courtyard nearby, leaning against the gnarled trunk of a banyan tree. "You didn't tell me Hugh was a tomcat," he said.

"What does that mean?"

"He had a yen for the fast life, nightclubs, strip joints."

"Not Hugh." She shook her head. "He's as solid as Gibraltar. If anything, he's a little straitlaced."

"Then what was he doing at Cheiro de Amor?"

She came immediately alert. "What's Cheiro de Amor? A nightclub? Did someone see him there? When?"

"He was seen there several nights, including the night before he disappeared. Not only that, Santeras owns the place."

"Let's go!"

"Hold on, Randy. The club is pretty racy. Are you sure?"

She dismissed the notion with a toss of her head.

"How racy could it be if Hugh went there? Of course I'm sure. When does it open?"

She was so eager and, as always, so damn sure of herself, Geoff had to subdue a smile. That's right, sweetness, he thought. Lead with your chin.

Randy had always had a notoriously active imagination. It was one of her survival skills as a child. A latchkey kid, stuck in a dingy apartment while her mother worked double shifts, she'd fed her soul on dreams and fantasies, many of them inspired by Edna—Cinderella stories with lavish balls, beautiful gowns, and of course, a handsome prince waiting in the wings.

Tonight she felt stirrings of that childhood magic as she stepped in front of the wardrobe mirror to look at herself. Her dark hair was piled high on her head in a sexy heap, her crystal earrings nearly touched her bare shoulders, and her dress was simple, yet elegant, a glittery white slip-dress with rhinestone-studded straps. She had never been so aware of her own feminine appeal. Maybe it was the lights or the mirror or her own excitement, but she really did look . . . desirable.

Geoff had told her the nightclub Hugh frequented was having a black-tie ball in celebration of Carnaval, and somehow he had managed to get two tickets to the sold-out affair. She couldn't imagine how a club that required black tie of its customers could be as racy as he'd implied.

The grandfather clock in the suite's foyer, began to chime, and its low vibrant music reminded Randy that she was late. Hurriedly she reached for her evening bag and the feathery white mask lying on the vanity.

Preoccupied with her mask and bag, she opened the bedroom door and walked into the suite's main salon. She knew Geoff would probably be waiting for her, and she hoped he wasn't the impatient type. But she wasn't in any way prepared for the sight that greeted her when she looked up.

"Oh, am I late?" she breathed softly. "I'm . . . sorry."

He was standing by the grand piano, a drink in hand, which he set down as she entered. He looked more expectant than impatient. But even if Randy, with all of her penchant for fairy tales, had tried to fantasize what Geoff Dias would look like in black tie, she couldn't have done him justice. He was fabulous, mouth-watering.

An element of surprise quivered in the sultry evening air as they stood across the room from each other, neither moving for a moment, both struck by what they saw. Geoff's gaze moved over her as if he could actually see the inner radiance she felt, as if he were taking measure of her in a whole new way.

But Randy was barely aware that she was being surveyed. She was too amazed by his transformation. How could a mercenary with holes in his fatigues have metamorphosed so perfectly into a prince? Geoff Dias looked as if he'd been born to the role. The severe lines of the tuxedo streamlined his body, lending a fashionable leanness to his powerful physique. Even his storm-blown blond hair was the perfect accent to the stark black-and-white formal wear. It spilled around his shoulders in a white-gold cascade that contrasted dramatically with his suntanned skin and his emerald green eyes.

He might as well have stepped out of a dream, full-blown, Randy admitted to herself secretly. Her dream.

"You don't have anything to be sorry for," he assured her, his voice resonant, full of male nuances. "Can I get you a drink?"

"Yes, thank you . . . whatever you're having."

He went to the sideboard and poured two fingers of Scotch from a crystal decanter, then added ice to the glass.

His back was to her, but Randy felt a little dizzy as she walked toward him, as if she were entering a force field that had risen up between them. Something made her want to hang back; perhaps it was the way her thoughts were racing. She was awash with anticipation, but she had no clear idea what she expected.

He startled her when he turned around. She was close enough to take the glass from his hand, and if their fingers hadn't brushed, she might never have let out the surprised, apologetic sound. As it was she jerked back as if he'd burned her, and there was no way to recover gracefully. She could feel herself blushing as she tried to smile and shrug it off. "It's all right," she said, glancing at him as she took the drink. "I'm fine."

Their gazes collided with almost physical force. Her head was tilted back slightly, and as she looked up at him, she knew it was going to be virtually impossible to tear herself away. His eyes were sinfully beautiful, so rich and verdant there was almost nothing she could do but gaze back at him. She could feel the pull of his interest all through her, tugging on her in deep and vibrant ways. Even her throat felt as if it were quivering. The perturbations were similar to those buzzing inside her when she'd been on his bike, but finer, much more exquisite.

It amazed her that he could bring her such pleasure with an accidental touch. Were her nerves that taut? One stroke and it felt as if they would resonate forever, like the strings on the beach troubadours' mandolins.

As though Randy's thoughts had summoned it, faint strains of music swirled up, drifting through their open terrace doors from somewhere in the near distance. Within seconds the music had grown louder and the beat more frenzied and insistent, pulling her attention away from the man standing before her. A raucous shriek of laughter made her start.

"What was that?" she asked, turning toward the doors.

"Carnaval. The parades must have started."

Geoff walked to the doors and shut them, muffling the sounds, but the intrusion of reality had done its job. The element of surprise that had held both of them spellbound was gone. Only the tension remained, a high-pitched awareness of each other that increased as he turned back to her.

"Is the drink all right?" he asked.

"Yes, I'm sure it's fine." She took a sip, hoping the icy liquor would slow her pulse. In the silence that followed, she began to realize what her nerves were all about. She'd had years to build a resistance to rough-and-ready biker types. Thanks to Edna, she had a natural immunity to rogues. But a rogue in a tuxedo? She hadn't been prepared for that combination. It must have been the sight of Geoff Dias in black tie, looking amazingly sexy and aristocratic at the same time, that had temporarily stripped her of her defenses.

"Whenever you're ready," he said. "Cheiro de Amor awaits."

"Yes, let's go." She was glad to be on their way. Given how the night had started, she was looking forward to the distractions of a black-tie party—and especially the safety of a crowd.

Eight

So this is Cheiro de Amor, Randy thought, thoroughly surprised and enchanted by the old-world Viennese elegance of the nightclub. Just moments before, she and Geoff had walked through the club's front doors and into a world of sparkling chandeliers and ornate candelabras. The gilded extravagance of the baroque decor was breathtaking, including lush red velvet draperies and crystal figurines that resembled bacchanalian maidens. If she hadn't known she was in the tropics, she might have thought she'd wandered into a European opera house. The place was almost decadent, it was so opulent.

No, it *was* decadent, she decided in the next breath, noticing the scanty French-maid outfits the hostesses were wearing. The one who greeted her and Geoff looked as if she'd misplaced her panties. More like an old-world bawdy house than an opera house, Randy decided as she and Geoff followed a particularly voluptuous Carioca hostess to a table for two near a heavily draped stage.

The sensual Latin music was a little disorienting too, Randy had to admit. One expected to hear a Strauss waltz instead of the low-pitched tribal drumbeats of a "dirty dance" like the lambada. As elegant as the place was, it fairly throbbed with an earthy and mysterious sexual quality.

All in all, Randy was intrigued. She'd only caught fleeting glimpses of the club's other patrons as she and Geoff moved through the low-lit ambience to their table. Some had been in black tie, others in more elaborate costumes. All wore masks, which created a faintly ominous aspect that might have concerned her more if it hadn't been Carnaval. Still, there was a sense of foreboding in the dark mood of the room.

Even her companion appeared somewhat sinister as she glanced at him across their table. Geoff was un-usually quiet as he returned her gaze, as if he were evaluating something about her. Too quiet, she de-cided. The black domino mask he wore drew attention to his eyes and shadowed his face, playing dramatic tricks with his features. It carved hollows beneath his cheekbones, and the sensual line of his lower lip seemed to whisper of a hidden capacity for both ten-derness and cruelty. He could have been one of Satan's disciples, if not the Prince of Darkness himself.

Randy touched one of the graceful white feathers of her own mask and looked around the room, suddenly very curious about what sort of club it was. "What does *cheiro de amor* mean?" she asked Geoff.

He drew a long-stemmed red rose out of the bud vase on their table and handed it to her, a suggestion of a smile on his lips. "The smell of love," he said.

"The rose, you mean?" She brought the petals to her nose and breathed in a musky, clinging fragrance that couldn't have been the rose's natural scent.

"No, I mean the club. It's called the smell of love."

"*Smell*?" Randy repeated the word, certain she couldn't possibly have heard him right. She glanced furtively at the rose, then returned it to the vase, posthaste.

Before she could question Geoff any further, their

French maid arrived with a bucket of iced champagne and two *batidas*, Brazilian drinks made of guava nectar, green lemon juice, and *cachaça*, a fiery sugarcane liqueur. One sip and Randy decided the drink's popularity was based on potency rather than taste. It had the kick of a twenty-mule team.

Geoff briefly conversed with the waitress in Portuguese, apparently asking her to run a tab. Randy began to fish through her purse, planning to show the woman Hugh's picture, but Geoff signaled her to hold off with a quick shake of his head.

The brassy sounds of a bossa nova drew Randy's attention to the opposite end of the room where a small live orchestra played on a balcony that was suspended from the wall above the dance floor. The dancers below wriggled and writhed with abandon, some of the women wearing little more than *tanga*. The men wore a variety of outfits, mostly fiendish in nature. Devils abounded in red tights, tails, and horns.

Randy didn't know whether to be amused or appalled. It looked like something out of Dante's *Inferno*. One gyrating woman appeared to be wearing nothing more than a sheer black body stocking with budding roses hiding the nipples of her breasts and a necklace of roses adorning her bottom like a G-string. The only other rose on her was dead center over her navel.

Her partner was also dressed in form-fitting black, but his mask was an elaborate affair that included a black mane of hair and wolf's ears. The two of them didn't dance so much as circle, twirling and sniffing like two wild creatures engaging in a mating ritual.

"Are you sure this was the club Hugh came to?" Randy asked Geoff, trying to imagine her fiancé in such a place.

"According to the cabbie, he might as well have lived here."

Randy shook her head, unable to take it in. Not only couldn't she imagine Hugh in a flesh palace like Cheiro de Amor, she'd often wondered if he might be under-sexed. When she'd told him she wanted to wait until they were married, he hadn't pressed her as most men would have. He'd always been patient and understanding.

Could Hugh have had a whole other life she knew nothing about? Randy helped herself to another drink of her *batida*, a deep pull this time. None of this made sense, but then nothing in her life had since Geoff Dias showed up. Maybe he'd kidnapped Hugh, she thought fancifully, taking the scenario to its absurd extremes. It was odd how Geoff had turned up just after Hugh disappeared. But then the ad she'd placed explained that . . . didn't it?

She felt something brush her hand and turned back to Geoff. His fingertips just touched hers, and she was struck with how ruggedly beautiful his hands were, how much latent male power they conveyed. The backs were large and strong, roped with tendons, burned by the sun. But his fingers revealed a different man. They were extraordinarily long and sensual, imbued with the sensitivity and fine-motor control of an artist. Stranger yet, his nails looked as if they weren't entirely unfamiliar with a manicurist's file. Artist, biker, or mercenary? she wondered. His hands were full of contradictions, like him.

"As long as we have the champagne . . ." he said, taking the bottle from the bucket. He filled two flutes and handed Randy one. "To Carnaval," he said, touching his glass to hers. "A feast for the senses."

"To Carnaval," Randy echoed. She'd always loved champagne. As she sipped it she relished the crisp dry taste and the geyser of bubbles that tickled her lips. The wine began to have a mellowing effect almost immediately, and she settled back into her chair, relaxing a bit. "Shouldn't we be making inquiries about Hugh?" she asked, feeling vaguely guilty about enjoying herself.

"We will," Geoff assured her. "Once I've had a chance to get the lay of this place, I'll ask some questions. In the meantime, enjoy the show." He nodded toward the dance floor.

Randy turned to look. The woman in the body stocking seemed to be conducting a one-woman floor show. She'd abandoned the wolf, and she was flirting madly with every demon, devil, and gargoyle in sight. Randy felt a moment of alarm when the woman began dancing her way toward their table. She apparently had Geoff in mind for her next conquest, and Randy wanted to trip her as she wriggled past.

Much to Randy's relief, Geoff shook his head when the woman tried to induce him to dance with her. Undaunted, she writhed sinuously around his chair, playing with his mask and his hair, slinking up behind him to nuzzle his neck. With amazing suppleness, she arched her spine over the back of his chair and stroked his ear with her tongue like a cat lapping cream. A moment later she'd come around the other side of the chair and was curling into his lap, rubbing her nearly naked body all over him.

Randy's shock turned to indignation as the woman entwined her arms around his neck, clearly intending to kiss him. The rest of it was theatrics, but a kiss, that was just too damn intimate. Randy's jaw began to ache, and she realized with surprise that she was clenching it. Why was Geoff allowing the woman to maul him? Why didn't he put a stop to it?

Randy rose in a huff, looking for the ladies' room, and collided with catwoman's partner. "Excuse me," Randy said, assuming the wolfman was on his way to collect his promiscuous partner—and perhaps punch Geoff in the eye. Randy wouldn't have minded either at that moment.

But the wolfman had other things in mind.

He slipped his hand around Randy's waist and slowly drew her against him. His muscular body was encased in dancerlike black tights, and his black mesh tank top revealed a triangle of chest hair that streaked all the way to his belly button. His eyes glowed luminously through the holes of his mask.

"You like to dance?" he asked, swaying to the beat of the pulsing music. His voice was as mellifluous as a samba and rife with Latin inflections.

Randy had every intention of turning him down. But as she glanced over her shoulder and saw Geoff still entangled with the catwoman, she decided she would like nothing better than to dance. She accepted with a flirty bat of her eyelashes, and the wolfman wasted no time splaying his hand over her derriere and drawing her into the orbit of his rotating pelvis.

"You do the forbidden dance?" he asked, urging her to move with him.

"If it's forbidden," she told him boldly, "I do it."

His hand tightened possessively on her bottom. Staring into her eyes, he began to swivel even more seductively, cranking her around with him. If they'd been churning butter, Randy decided, they would have had a bucket by now. "Couldn't we spin or something?" she asked.

"*Ôba!*" he said, an ecstatic groan in his voice.

Randy assumed that must be Portuguese for "spin," because he began to twirl her around madly. She managed to catch a glance of Geoff as she turned, and saw with great satisfaction that she had his attention at last. He didn't look happy, she noted. Neither did the catwoman, who'd been ejected from his lap.

"*Ôba, ôba!*" the wolfman cried again.

Ôba or not, Randy was ready to land. The spinning was making her dizzy and her heart was beginning to pound. But how to get that across to her highly enthusiastic partner? She tried to free her hand, but he seemed to be misreading her signals. He whipped her into his arms and bent her over backward, gripping her by the waist with both hands and shaking her out like a throw rug. Even upside down, Randy could see the jealous fire building in Geoff's eyes.

"Don't!" Randy squealed as the wolfman ran his hands up her rib cage, tickling a scream out of her. She couldn't help herself. There were certain vulnerable spots on her body that sent her into nearly hysterical fits. Unfortunately, her squeals seemed to incite the wolfman.

"*Ôba!*" he groaned, his hands all over her.

"Stop!" she shrieked, trying to get up.

Geoff rose from his chair, full of menace. Randy saw him coming. She also saw the darkening fury of his intention, but there wasn't time to warn the wolfman. There wasn't time for anything! She was jerked up to a vertical position as her partner was ripped bodily from her arms.

"May I cut in?" Geoff asked, lethally polite. He'd picked the wolfman up by his armpits and was holding him suspended in the air.

"No!" Randy exclaimed. But to her dismay, the wolfman was frantically nodding yes. "Put him down, Geoff," she ordered, a little discouraged at the wolfman's lack of gallantry. Weren't Latin men supposed to be famous for their displays of machismo? At the very least she would like to have seen some foot-stamping or chin-thrusting. Instead, the moment the wolfman's feet touched the ground, he shot off as if hounds were at his heels.

"I'm not sure I want to dance with you," Randy informed Geoff, favoring him with her version of an upthrust chin. She cocked her head and shot him a look that said "Buzz off, buster."

It worked better than she'd expected. His eyes ignited, flaring inside the black mask with a warning that made Randy catch her breath and step back. If there was a man alive capable of breathing fire, Geoff Dias was that man, she realized.

"Maybe I can help you make up your mind," he said, closing the distance she'd put between them. He searched her face as if he meant to devour her, and then he placed his hand exactly where her former partner's had been, on the rounded curve of her derriere. "You seemed to like this when *he* did it."

"I did like it," she lied.

His fingers sank into her flesh, and his thumb closed over her hipbone. "Wrong answer, sweetness," he said roughly. "You're not allowed to like it with anyone else. Not with him, not with Hugh, not with anybody but me."

He stared into her eyes, his fingers tensing, relaxing. And then he began to work his hand slowly, massaging her derriere in ways that made Randy's muscles grip and ache. The shock of it heated her blood to a low flame and sent a languorous weakness spilling through her veins. The shock of it thrilled her. She tried to protest, but he pressed his other hand to her mouth, silencing her with long, long fingers.

Randy went still immediately, though she couldn't have explained why she was allowing him to handle her in such an intimate way. They were shadowed by darkness, and she doubted if the other patrons could see them, but still, they were in a public place. Yet something about the silent authority of his fingers on her mouth kept her motionless. Something about their pressure against the pliancy of her lips, their warmth and firmness.

She should have been fighting, but she could feel her lips tingling, responding in a way that made it seem as if she were kissing his fingertips, a willing victim. He pressed into her softness, seducing her with slow, hypnotic strokes, the way a cobra enthralls its prey.

When he seemed persuaded that she wouldn't put up a fight, he began to move his hand down her throat, slowly, creating a mesmerizing friction as he curved his palm to the lines of her neck, molded it to her collarbone and then drew it even lower, measuring the quick rise and fall of her breathing. Each touch was spellbinding in the way it made her anticipate the next one.

Her eyelids drooped, wanting to close as she memo-
rized the width of his palm and the length of his fingers.
He had rugged, beautiful hands. Artistic hands, gifted
with precision and sensitivity. She could already imagine them on her breasts, thrilling her, claiming her in
the same possessive way he was palming her bottom.

"Look at me, Randy."

She resisted until his fingers spoke to her, overriding
her will in a way that his sensual voice couldn't. She
looked up at him, her heart crowding her throat. He
was the kind of man who could make a woman do
anything, she realized. He could master a woman's
flesh with his hands and still the last quiver of defiance
in her soul. She should have been trying to find a way
to release herself from his power. Instead, she was
glorying in the weakness she felt.

When he seemed satisfied that he had her undivided
attention, he gave her the urgent thrill she'd been
imagining. He slipped his hand inside the bodice of her
dress and cupped her naked breast. The audacity of it
sent a shock of pleasure flowing all the way to the soles
of her feet.

"Nobody, baby," he whispered, giving her a possessive little shake with his hands. "Nobody but me."

Randy felt grounded to the floor by the painful currents of excitement running through her. Samba music
throbbed around her, hot and heavy, and the musky
perfume of roses was nearly suffocating as she
breathed it in. She swayed toward Geoff, drunk with
the sensations of the moment. He bent to kiss her and
as their lips touched, a kind of chaos broke out around
them. The room went wine red with light, and the
band's brass section launched into a fanfare of trum-
pets.

Bewildered, Randy noticed the curtain rising on the
stage next to their table. Apparently the show was
starting. Or were they the show? She glanced around

the room and saw all eyes trained in their direction. A flicker of amusement crossed Geoff's lips and Randy realized he wasn't embarrassed in the slightest. Like an incorrigible kid caught with his hand in the cookie jar, he seemed to be finding the situation quite entertaining.

Randy didn't share the sentiment. Furious, she slapped his hand away, then twisted around and straightened her dress. But if she was angry with him, she was even angrier with herself. How many kinds of idiot was she for getting herself into these predicaments with him? He took advantage again and again, but she couldn't seem to get it through her head that he was the enemy. He might be the only man who could find Hugh, but he was also the one man who could ruin her life!

She turned to the entrance, intending to get some air, and was alarmed to see a guard posted by the door.

"You might as well sit down," Geoff said, his hand on her waist. "They don't let people in or out during the floor show."

"Why?" she demanded. "Is it so bad, people try to escape?"

He merely smiled. "You'll see."

Randy sat down, still fuming. Her jaw ached like fire and she was already regretting her eagerness to check out the club. Some investigation this was turning out to be. They hadn't even asked about Hugh yet.

The band was going full tilt with the torchiest music imaginable when Randy finally got around to glancing at the stage. The set consisted of nothing more than a streetlamp with a smoldering Latin male leaning against it. A female temptress, writhing to the music behind him, was tugging his white T-shirt out of his jeans and brushing herself up against his backside.

For all of the woman's diligence, she didn't look as if she wanted to do his laundry, Randy decided. The straps of her sliplike dress were hanging off her shoulders, and her breasts strained against the sheer material. She was wanton seduction itself, yet somehow the man managed to feign indifference, even as she pulled up his shirt and exposed his muscled chest to her roaming hands.

Feigned was the key word, Randy realized when she noticed the burgeoning in the man's pants. That wasn't supposed to happen in floor shows, was it? The woman began to unbuckle his belt, brazen in her eagerness to touch him. As she unzipped his fly, the man glanced down, watching her hands work their seductive magic.

Randy looked away, as startled by the act as the memory it evoked. It forced her to think about what she'd done to Geoff that night years ago. She shifted in the chair and rearranged herself, crossing her legs and tugging down her skirt. But nothing she did could stop the flood of images or the soft aching that stirred inside her. Some experiences were indelible, so sharply engraved on the nervous system, they could never be erased. That night was everywhere, past flowing into the present like an erupting volcano.

The music hit a resounding crescendo. As Randy looked up, bongo drums throbbed and the man on the stage came alive. He grasped the woman's hand and swung her around in front of him, bringing her to her knees in an erotic, dancelike move.

Seemingly crazed with desire, the woman strained toward him, letting out an anguished moan as he pulled her to her feet and pressed her to the back wall of the shallow stage. As she writhed against his imprisoning hands, her dress inched down her shoulders, freeing one of her breasts to the man's gaze, and to his mouth as he bent to taste her.

It all happened so quickly, Randy couldn't look away. Her breathing went high and shallow, coming from some tight corner of her throat. These people weren't playacting, she realized as the man tangled his hands in the woman's skirt and drew the silk up her thighs.

Unable to free herself, Randy felt a sickening flash of shock and excitement as she watched the erotic spectacle. The dancers' naked desire left her dizzy and fighting to breathe. She glanced at Geoff and saw a glint of green through his black mask. He'd been watching *her* rather than the show, she realized. But for how long? He looked sinister now, like some kind of demon god presiding over the festivities. His gaze made her feel like a sacrificial virgin being primed for her own ravishment.

A screech of laughter struck at Randy's fraying nerves. She came out of the chair, bewildered, frightened. As she pulled off her mask, she noticed the furtive eyes of the crowd glancing her way. Their smiles seemed to taunt her and leer, and the blaring orchestra music throbbed in her head. Had she gone crazy or was everyone in the room watching her with some kind of demonic amusement?

Panic galvanized her. She started for the entrance, her only thought to get out of the room. The guard was so absorbed in the show, he made no attempt to stop her as she rushed past him. She burst through the door to the club's foyer and then out the next door to an even more chaotic scene—tribal drums, samba bands, and careening floats.

Clowns teetered by on towering stilts, nearly naked women quivered blissfully to the music, and conga lines of revelers danced in the streets, whirling dervishes of primal energy and sensuality. It was Carnaval, Randy realized. There was no escaping the madness!

Someone jostled her from behind, and she stumbled forward toward the street. Before she could catch her balance, a grinning Dracula caught hold of her hand and dragged her with him into a conga line. She was swept along with the crowd, sucked deeper and deeper into the frenzied crush.

Costumed bodies slammed into her, anonymous

hands groped her, and the musk of overheated human flesh assailed her senses. A heel snapped off her shoe and one of her shoulder straps tore free of its moorings. She clutched the bodice of her dress as she fought to stay on her feet. It was raw fear that kept her going. The only rule was survival—move with the teeming masses or be trampled by them.

"Randy!"

She heard Geoff's voice through the din, but she couldn't see him. As the parade swung around a corner, the pack that surrounded her became even more compressed. For several seconds, she was lifted off the ground as the press of bodies threatened to crush the wind out of her. "Geoff!" she screamed in terror.

Another shift in the parade's direction dropped her to the ground like a rock. Her feet collided with the pavement and she pitched forward, landing on one knee. Pain jolted through her as revelers swarmed around her, knocking her off balance again and again.

"Randy! Here!"

She heard Geoff calling to her and as she fought to get up, then strong hands lifted her free of the melee. A moment later he was pulling her with him into the safety of a narrow alleyway, drawing her into a recessed doorway.

She'd never been so glad to see anyone in her life. Sobbing with relief, she threw her arms around him and buried her face in his hair. He held her protectively, cradling her head in the curve of his throat. "Randy, Randy," he crooned harshly, "don't ever do anything crazy like that again. You could have gotten yourself killed."

For once Randy hadn't the slightest inclination to argue with him. It felt too good being safe in his arms. It felt like heaven after the nightmare of purgatory. And that was all she wanted for now, just the solace of being held and stroked and loved until she could stop shaking.

Loved? she thought . . . loved? Was that what she wanted?

Yes, just for now.

He seemed to understand her need. The sheltering strength of his arms conveyed that he had no intention of letting her go until she was ready. If she wanted to be held until the sun ceased to shine, he'd be there.

For Randy it was a new experience. She'd never let herself receive comfort from a man before, simply taking what was offered. She'd always thought women had to barter with men, as her mother had: An act of sex equaled some affection; tears were good for an apology; a hint of contrition, maybe even dinner. It was all coercion, giving to get. But this kindness felt blissfully undeserved. She'd given Geoff Dias nothing but grief so far.

It took her some time, but finally she was able to separate herself from the muscled warmth of his body long enough to glance up at him. "I think I'm going to live," she told him.

"I'm glad to hear it." He continued to smooth her hair as if that were his sole purpose in life. "Why did you run away?"

"I had to." She was surprised he didn't understand. "That floor show! And you, the Prince of Darkness himself, leering at me like I was some kind of virgin sacrifice—or a peach ripening to be plucked."

His expression was one of droll self-restraint. "You have quite an imagination, lady."

"Don't lie. You weren't thinking about plucking me?"

"I think about that a lot, but I'd rather do it privately, just the two of us. Say . . . back at the hotel? It's short notice for a virgin sacrifice, but I'll see what I can do. Of course, we'll need a virgin."

"Cheeky bastard," she said, laughter bubbling in her reproach. Still suspicious of his sexy grin, she leaned back, letting herself be supported by the circle of his arms. "You had no ulterior motives in mind taking me to the club?"

"Randy, *you* insisted on going." He lifted the dangling rhinestone strap of her dress, drawing the bodice up to cover the creamy fullness of one nearly exposed breast. "If I had ulterior motives, would I be doing this?"

He'd picked the wrong area of her body to be gallant about, especially considering the liberties he'd taken earlier—and in his office. "Don't play games with me, Geoff Dias," she warned, surprised at the emotion in her voice. "I'm not an easy mark, whatever evidence you may think you have to the contrary. I won't be trifled with like all those other women you've conquered—the 'babies' on your bike."

She pressed her hands to his biceps and pushed, making a halfhearted attempt to extricate herself. He countered by slipping his fingers into her hair, by stroking the tautness below her cheekbone with his thumb. Finally, reluctantly, she met his eyes and felt her pulse rate soar.

"I'm not trifling," he insisted quietly. "If I wanted to trifle, I could have had that crazed woman back at Cheiro de Amor. And the 'baby' on my bike is singular, just one woman."

His voice dropped low, but there was something passionate in its tone, something male and possessive. "It's you . . . Randy. Baby, it's you."

Randy was more than astonished, she was fearful. He'd sounded as if he meant it. But surely that was impossible. Men like Geoff Dias didn't squander themselves on just one female, not with so much testosterone to spread around, not with so many worlds to conquer, so many women. "What are you saying?" she demanded, covering her alarm with questions. "What do you mean, it's me?"

He shook his head, as if a little confused himself. "I don't know, maybe I want to give this thing a chance.

See what happens—if anything *can* happen between us."

Randy was shaken by the way her blood was rushing and her mind was racing. She didn't want to hear what he was saying to her, and yet she didn't want him to stop. *Give this thing a chance?* God, how that idea frightened her. It was impossible.

"No, I can't take chances, Geoff," she told him. "I need something solid. I *have* something solid."

He tipped up her chin and stared at her hard. "Right, you've got a solid guy who hangs out at places called The Smell of Love?"

"Oh—and you don't hang out at places like that?"

"Sure I do, but I admit to it, Randy. I'm not pretending to be Mr. Clean. I'm not lying to you."

"What's that supposed to mean?" she asked him. "That Hugh *is* lying to me? About what?" She could hardly believe it. Geoff Dias was setting himself up as morally superior to her fiancé? The man who rode bikes like a banshee and carried a flask in his hip pocket? Hugh was a fine man, a conscientious man who'd worked his whole life to get where he was.

"There are plenty of things your fiancé could be lying about," Geoff pointed out. "Like what he was doing at that nightclub, why he met with Santeras."

She met his emerald gaze head on. "Are you asking me to believe that Hugh was doing something wrong, something illegal?"

"I'm not asking you to believe anything about Hugh. I'm telling you something about me. I've never lied to you, and I never will. Maybe you're not used to that in a man."

Randy had a moment of true confusion. His thumb was still stroking her face lightly, and the conviction in his voice pulled at her. It reached into her mind and made her want to question the things she'd taken for granted as true. He seemed to be saying he wanted a relationship with her. But maybe he was just playing with her head, her hopes, trying to convince her that he was a man who didn't lie, a man who would hold her simply because she needed holding. But why would he do all that? What was his motive? Surely he had one. All men did.

He bent to kiss her and she whispered something as his mouth neared hers. "Is the deal off, then? The night of sex?"

"No, sweetness," he said, tasting her lips, sipping, sampling, tantalizing, "the deal isn't off. You're not going to leave Hugh for me. You're too frightened. And if I can't have anything else, then I want that night. *I mean to have that night.*"

His lips continued to touch hers, light, sexy, wickedly sweet. His hand went to the breast he'd covered, and she felt a shock wave of desire as his skin touched her bare flesh. He was right. Everything he said was true. She wasn't going to leave Hugh, she couldn't. It would kill her to give up her dreams.

But there was one thing Geoff Dias didn't know, must never know. She wanted that night of sex with him. She wanted it badly.

Nine

Geoff, wearing only his tuxedo pants, stood alone in the darkness of his bedroom gazing out the open terrace doors. The low vibrant music of the grandfather clock echoed from the foyer, followed by four lonely chimes. The sound was haunting. Even the chaos of Carnaval, roiling up on sultry waves of heat, couldn't offset the sad beauty of the chimes.

They reminded him of her.

He'd been sketching her in his mind again, the gypsy bride in her lacy white wedding gown and her shattered dreams. It was the same image, always the same, her eyelashes quivering with tears, her features suffused with a young girl's pain, a young woman's stung pride.

Why did he always think of her that way? There were a million other images that could have obsessed him— their white-hot coupling on the bike, their abandoned sex in the roadside motel he'd found. She'd been crazy enough to try everything that night, perhaps a little too desperate. At one point she'd thrown herself against the wall, facing away from him, begging him to take her that way. And then in the heat of it, before either of them were finished, she'd freed herself and knelt before him, bringing him to the most explosive climax he'd ever had.

His gut knotted up violently with the memory. Aware of the heat pooling in his groin, he went to the dresser and poured himself a splash of brandy from a crystal decanter. That session had sure as hell left an impression on him. Why couldn't he draw it? Why did he keep re-creating a sad and beautiful child-woman, full of melancholy, shadowed with yearnings?

Why couldn't he get her out of his system?

He walked out onto the terrace, drink in hand, barely aware of the sweltering heat. There was an aching sensation between his ribs that intensified whenever he took a breath. It was associated with her, he knew, and it would only get worse. She was slowly but surely driving him nuts. She could have been crushed in that mob scene, and the thought of losing her that way had churned up feelings. It had made him realize that he cared about her, maybe even enough to think about the consequences of hurting her.

He took a quick slug of the brandy and grimaced as it set fire to the roof of his mouth. If he were a better man, he'd find her Prince Charming for her and get out of her life. There was no way to get the satisfaction he wanted from her short of destroying her dream. If she wanted a loveless marriage to a buttoned-down desk jockey— permanence over passion—that was her choice.

He glanced down at her balcony and saw that the doors to her room were open. Something tugged deep inside him, tempting him to think of it as an invitation. Hell, she'd invited him in the club, surrendering her mouth to him, her breast, then pulling back abruptly when they were interrupted. He wanted to believe that if they'd been somewhere else, with nothing to stop them, she would have surrendered it all.

He drained the rest of the brandy in his glass, fighting fire with fire, trying to put out the blaze in his gut. If he were a better man, he wouldn't even be thinking about such things. If he were a better man . . .

Where had he gone? Randy crumpled the note she'd found on her pillow that morning and tossed it into the basin of a green marble birdbath that stood in the midst of the terrace garden. With a sigh of frustration, she picked up her dripping glass of iced tea and took a drink, ignoring the fruit salad that sat on the table next to her.

Geoff had already gone out when she'd awakened at eight A.M., and his terse message said he'd left to investigate a new lead. It gave no specifics, not even an estimate of the time he'd be back. She glanced at her watch, then chided herself because she'd checked it just moments before.

It was well past noon now, and she was becoming increasingly uneasy—not only about what he was doing, but about what they'd done the night before. She'd had wild dreams the entire night, all of them dominated by an emerald-eyed devil in a black mask. She'd awakened in turmoil, determined to talk to him about their "problem"—and found him gone.

Aware of the dull throb above her eye, which always signaled the beginning of a headache, she rose and walked to the railing. She'd called room service twice for aspirin, but no one had ever shown up. It seemed a miracle they'd brought lunch, considering the chaos that had taken hold of the city.

A cluster of vermilion butterflies swooped overhead and doubled back, alighting on the crimson bougainvillea that grew along the railing. Randy was struck by the natural beauty of Rio as she gazed out at the seascape, at Sugarloaf Mountain and the white puff clouds drifting above. On impulse she decided to take a walk. The exercise would relax her, and she might find a pharmacy in one of the shops nearby where she could get some aspirin.

A short time later she was traversing a shady side street, picking her way through streamers, confetti, and the other paraphernalia of last night's celebration. In the near distance she could hear the roar of the official parades, where samba schools from all over Brazil were competing for the enormous prestige of taking first place in the dance competition.

Making a mental note of her surroundings so she could find her way back, she took a street heading in the opposite direction from the parades. She wanted to avoid the crowds.

Most of the shops were closed, but she was hoping to come across a grocery or drugstore. She covered a few blocks, took another corner and heard the soft purr of a car engine. Glancing behind her, she noticed a sleek black limo as it gingerly negotiated the turn and crept into a parking spot.

The luxury car looked out of place among the modest shops and businesses. Randy glanced back again curiously, but she was unable to see anything through the tinted windows.

As she continued on down the street, a crazy quilt of multicolored shacks in the distance caught her eye. Clustered precariously on a hillside, they spilled down to the very edge of the business district. Her guidebook had warned that the shanty towns of Rio, called *favelas*, were dangerous. They were the poverty pockets of the city, where criminals and drug pushers hung out. They were also home to the poor and underprivileged.

Randy continued walking, drawn by a group of children who were sitting on a sidewalk in front of a shop window. They were watching a television set through the glass, and Randy's heart went out to them as she neared. Thin and ragged, they sat clutching their knees, completely absorbed by the old western movie.

Down the street on the opposite corner was an open-air stand of fruits and vegetables. Randy's first thought was to buy the children some food, but as she stepped into the street she became aware of a man loitering near a streetlamp by the stand. He leaned against the post, watching her and looking vaguely sinister, not unlike the dancer who'd performed at the club the night before.

Randy told herself to keep going. It was daylight and there were people around. She'd be safe enough. Her attention divided between the man and the produce, she approached the stand and picked out a variety of fresh fruits, avoiding the milk chocolate candy the owner was pointing out to her. She didn't want the children to gorge on sweets and become ill.

The shopkeeper's thick accent made his words unintelligible, but he seemed more than happy to take Randy's American money, and she was sure that she must have overpaid by the delighted smile on his face. She returned his smile as she took the bag. It pleased her to think that she was helping in some way.

But as she turned to leave, she immediately sensed the danger. Three men were now congregated at the streetlamp, and two more were crossing the street from the direction she'd come. Not only were they blocking her path, they were heading straight for her.

One of them called out something in Portuguese and the others laughed and jeered. Randy hesitated as all five began to move toward her, closing in. She knew it wouldn't do any good to scream. The streets were suddenly deserted. Even the old man who'd waited on her had disappeared.

Adrenaline burned through her hesitation. Raised in the streets herself, she'd learned some lessons in survival. She pulled an orange from the sack she carried and held it out as if offering it to the men blocking her path. "Catch!" she cried, tossing it to the nearest one.

She flung the bag of fruit at the other man and made a run for it.

The bluff gave her a few seconds' head start, and Randy dug in as she never had before. Raw fear propelled her forward. She heard the roar of a car's engine as she sprinted toward the end of the block. Suddenly the black limo peeled out of its parking space, drowning Randy's screams in the screech of its tires. It came right at her, forcing her to leap out of the way as it careened past. Astonished, she watched the big car swerve to a shuddering stop, blocking the path of her pursuers.

The limo door flew open. "Get in!" someone shouted.

It was a man's voice, but Randy couldn't see him. Torn, she looked up and spotted her pursuers climbing over the hood of the car after her.

"*Get in!*" the voice commanded.

Randy scrambled into the car. Blinded by the dark interior, she felt someone lean over her and pull the door shut. She shuddered and fell against the seat as the limo wheeled around. The car jumped over the curb and shot down the road, scattering the men who'd chased her.

"Thank you," Randy said, trying to discern the face of her rescuer. Her relief lessened the apprehension she felt, despite the fact that from what she could see of him, he looked every inch a dangerous man. He might have been in his forties, though it was hard to tell. His face was unlined, and his eyes were as dark as the hair that swirled to his shoulders in unruly waves.

He was certainly dressed to kill, she noted. He wore black, everywhere. His shirt and slacks appeared to be silk, and though they were loosely constructed, they fit him as if they'd been tailored on his body. But more riveting than anything else about him was the white scar that bisected his tanned throat as if someone had literally tried to cut it.

"Did they hurt you?" he asked, his voice inflected with nuances that were more European than Latin.

"No, they didn't catch me, thanks to you."

"You're American?"

"Yes, from California." She told him her name and explained that she was buying fruit for the children, then waited for him to introduce himself.

Instead, he studied her with apparent curiosity. "A good samaritan?" he observed. "I wonder if your charitable attempt was worth it. It nearly got you killed."

"I don't think of myself as a good samaritan," she countered, wondering if she should be offended by his comment. It seemed more an observation than a criticism. "The children looked hungry."

"And you were only trying to help, of course."

"Yes, actually, I was."

"Another of life's lessons, perhaps?" he wondered aloud. "But what does this one mean? That we should leave others to their fate and not interfere? Perhaps the only destiny we can affect is our own?"

Randy was sure she'd never had a stranger conversation. Her rescuer talked in riddles. "In that case you shouldn't have saved me," she pointed out. "It feels good doing something for someone else, don't you think? I'm only sorry the fruit was wasted."

He smiled, something she suspected he didn't often do. "I will see the children get their fruit," he said. "I will interfere in their fate as well as yours—if that is your wish."

The remark was heavy with unspoken meanings. Studying him, Randy was struck by the high-arcing bones and dusky skin tones that dominated his features. The arrogance was there, set into the strong angles of his face, as was the male pride of bearing so reminiscent of Latin cultures. But along with it, there was something shadowed about the man who'd rescued her, something unspoken, like his remark.

Still, she found herself wanting to take his offer in the spirit of goodwill. "Yes, please," she said at last. "I'd appreciate it."

"Where are you staying?" he asked.

She gave him the name of the hotel, and when they arrived at their destination just moments later, Randy was vaguely disappointed that the adventure was over so quickly. As the chauffeur opened her door she realized she didn't even know her rescuer's name.

"Please," he said, holding out a card as she turned to him. "Take this. And come to my party tonight. It's a masquerade ball, a charity event for the children of the *favelas.*"

"A charity event?" Randy read the card, which had only an address, no name. She glanced up at his mysterious smile.

"I'm an old hand at interfering in fate," he said.

Before she could ask him anything more, she felt the driver at her elbow, helping her out. His firm grip on her arm gave her no choice but to go.

Randy stood on the curb as the limo drove away, her head still buzzing from the odd encounter. "Do you know whose address this is?" she asked as the hotel doorman approached her. She handed him the card and saw by his startled expression that he did.

"Where did you get this?" he asked. "It's Carlos Santeras's jungle villa."

Randy didn't answer him. Her eyes riveted on the departing limo. "Carlos Santeras?"

The rest of the afternoon crawled by for Randy. Her excitement and frustration mounted as she waited for Geoff to return. She'd purchased a veiled and sequined harem outfit for the party in one of the hotel's shops, and now she was sitting on her bed in a short silk kimono, immersed in cosmetic rituals—curling her eyelashes, redoing her nails, and the like. She would need glamour to spare for Santeras's party tonight. The skimpy harem outfit would help, and she already had Greta Garbo eyebrows.

"Can anyone come to this slumber party?"

Randy glanced up, startled by the sight of Geoff Dias standing in the open doorway of her bedroom. The tuxedo and the black mask of the night before were long gone, distant memories. Now his golden hair was subdued by a black martial arts bandanna, and the shoulders that swelled from the straps of his military T-shirt were burned by the sun. He looked as if he'd been cruising the highways all day, a renegade biker, running on wind and adrenaline, searching for the ultimate high.

Struck by the way he could transform so totally, Randy flashed back to the soldier of fortune who'd stormed her office with his ripped fatigues and his silver flask filled with mystery elixir. Her heart moved strangely in her chest, just as it had then.

"Sorry, girls only," she said, turning her attention to the hot-pink toenail she'd started. Her hand was unsteady, and she had to concentrate fiercely to apply the remaining strokes. It didn't surprise her that she could respond to the mere sight of him. Considering what had happened between them, it would have been odd if she hadn't. She was disturbed because it was his wildness that had triggered the response.

"In that case the party's over," he said. "We've got to talk."

He strode to the bed and sat down, forcing a moan out of Randy as her hand went berserk. There was nail polish all over her foot! "Look there!" she snapped, shoving the brush back into the tiny bottle of polish and screwing the top shut. "Look what you've done. Where the hell are your manners, Dias?"

"PMS again?"

His faint grin sent her off on another tangent. "We had an agreement," she reminded him hotly, daubing at her toe with a tissue. "Or did you forget that I'm supposed to be calling the shots? Where were you all day?" It felt good giving him hell, she realized. She knew she was taking her frustrations out on him. But who better? He was the one who'd caused them.

"All I did was sit on the bed, Randy," he said softly. "If you want to bitch about something, bitch about this."

To her utter shock, he grabbed her by the ankles and dragged her down the bed toward him, ignoring her gasps as he pried open her legs and scooped her onto his lap.

All of the tension that had been building between them exploded as he buried his hand in her hair and kissed her soundly, his mouth hard and overpowering. Randy's scream got trapped in her throat. For an instant she was too stunned to react, and then she came to her senses with a burst. She twisted and shoved at him until he grasped her by the wrists and locked her hands behind her back.

The kiss turned hotly passionate then, Randy writhing against him in a rush of primitive arousal. She moaned and swore at him through her clenched teeth, unable to do anything to stop him, outraged at the way he'd taken control. God, the sounds she was making, so breathy and urgent, as if she liked what he was doing when she didn't! *She hated it.*

"Bitch about this," he murmured, nuzzling her throat and nipping the tender flesh beneath her chin.

The stinging sweetness of it drove Randy wild. She wrenched her hands free, arching up, swinging wildly, not even knowing what she was going to do. He caught her in midair, a body block as he threw her back down on the bed and loomed over her.

"All right," she cried, staring up at his flying golden hair and his blazing eyes, "do it! Go ahead, take me by force. You've probably always wanted to anyway."

He backed off for a second, breathing hard, then captured her wrists and pinned them above her head as if he'd accepted the challenge. *In a heartbeat, woman*, his expression said. *Just one heartbeat.* Randy didn't move, she didn't even breathe as he bent over her on all fours like a predatory animal. The sharp glare of his eyes penetrated her to the core.

A sound caught in her throat, more whimper than moan, and it was choked and trembly, rife with sexual urgency.

A knowing smile darkened his features. "Maybe we should be talking about what *you* want, hmm, Randy?"

He sat back on his haunches, resting his hands on his thighs as he studied the quickness of her breathing and the heat that mottled her throat. "Seems like there must be an easier way to have a conversation with you, woman. That was all I had in mind when I came in here."

Conversation? Randy was absolutely humming with sexual arousal. Her whole body was aquiver with it. "Then would you mind getting off me?" she suggested, wishing she could make her voice sharper and less shaky. "I converse better when I'm not being pinned to a bed."

By the time he'd rolled off her and Randy had her kimono tied securely around her, she'd calmed down a little. At least her thighs weren't quivering anymore. "What did you want to talk about?" she asked Geoff.

He was standing alongside the bed, watching her, his eyes simmering with unslaked desire. Why hadn't he made love to her? she wondered. She wouldn't have stopped him. She *couldn't* have stopped him. She didn't seem to have an OFF switch where he was concerned. Fortunately, he did. He seemed bent on proving he could control even the most overpowering needs.

"Your fiancé," he said. "I turned up something this morning."

"What is it? Tell me!"

Clearly in no hurry, Geoff pulled the silver flask from the back pocket of his fatigue pants, removed the cap, and took a swig. "Have some?" he asked, offering the flask to her. "It's good for whatever ails you. Kills it dead"

"If that's true, then you should be keeling over any minute."

He tossed the flask on the bed, apparently thinking she might change her mind, then walked to the balcony doors. A cloud of moist heat billowed in and he opened them. "Hugh tried to charter a private plane to São Paulo last week. He wanted to leave that day, but the guy couldn't take him, so he left."

Randy felt a swift, draining relief as she realized that someone had seen Hugh. He was alive. "Maybe he used another charter?"

"No, I checked the others—car rentals and bus depots, everything. No one recognized Hugh's picture. It's possible somebody was holding out. As you already know, locals don't like to get involved in investigations."

Randy sat forward, clutching at the gaping neckline of her kimono. "But what if they're not holding out? Maybe Hugh was trying to get out of the city and couldn't? What if he's still here, trapped somewhere, hiding from Santeras? What—" She broke off, her thoughts racing ahead of her words. "What if he's being held by Santeras?"

Geoff's expression said he wasn't impressed with her idea. "If Santeras wanted Hugh out of the picture, there are more efficient ways."

"But didn't you tell me you'd rescued an agent from Santeras's converted slave quarters? It's worth checking out, isn't it?" She'd left the card Santeras had given her on the nightstand next to the bed. "I met him this afternoon, and he invited me to a party tonight."

"You met Carlos Santeras? How did that happen?"

Randy explained hurriedly, handing Geoff the card.

"Good God," he said, reading Santeras's address aloud. "You're a magnet for trouble, woman. It's a wonder you're still around to paint your toenails."

He tucked the card in his pocket and flashed her a warning glare when she protested. "I'll check out the party," he announced firmly. "Our deal was that you'd stay in the hotel if things got dangerous. They just got dangerous."

"Geoff! It's a party! How dangerous could that be?"

"If Hugh's on the run and Santeras wants him, then you'd be the perfect bait. Do you think it's a coincidence he was there today in his limo? He may have you under surveillance. No, you're not leaving this room, not until I can put you on a plane back to the States."

Fighting the desire to argue with him, Randy began to reinspect the damage to her toenails. "*Fine*," she said, knowing it was pointless to try to change his mind. "Have fun at the party. Why don't you go as the Terminator? You won't need an outfit."

"What I need is a drink," Geoff said, scooping the flask off the bed and stashing it in his back pocket as he strode out of her bedroom.

Randy began to perspire as he disappeared through her doorway. Her reaction had nothing to do with the heat and humidity and everything to do with the decision she'd just made. She was going to the party. She was a woman who believed in opportunity, and this one was twenty-four-carat gold. It wasn't as if she was breaking her bargain with Geoff, not technically. She simply didn't agree with his definition of dangerous. Santeras wouldn't know who she was in the harem outfit, not unless she chose to tell him. And of course, Geoff Dias wouldn't recognize her either.

Ten

Carlos Santeras's jungle villa wasn't exactly on the bus route, Randy realized as the taxi she'd taken snaked along a winding road that climbed to the crest of a forested mountain. The doorman at the hotel had given the taxi driver instructions and paid him in advance, so Randy was reasonably sure she wasn't being hijacked into white slavery. On the other hand, the doorman had also mentioned the mansion's converted subterranean slave quarters, though he hadn't said what they were converted into. Randy intended to find out.

The taxi slowed at a gated entrance, and once they sped through, she was treated to a breathtaking drive through exotic terraced gardens and water isles, all softly spotlighted. The trees were strung with enough twinkling lights to rival a far-flung galaxy of stars. By night the grounds were a fairyland of pure enchantment.

Randy leaned forward, touching the car's window as Santeras's Mediterranean-style villa came into view. The magnificent white-columned mansion was aglow, and every kind of luxury car imaginable crowded the curved driveway. As the taxi swept up to the entrance, she looked around for Geoff's Harley, but didn't spot it.

"Madame?" The rich, musical voice belonged to an

exceedingly tall footman whose snowy white morning coat contrasted beautifully with his ebony skin. He opened the taxi door and helped her out, spiriting her up the front steps and through a marble foyer that opened onto an atrium with bubbling fountains. A cathedral-ceilinged ballroom lay just beyond, apparently the glittering centerpiece of the mansion.

"Thank you," Randy told the doorman as he left her at the entrance to the ballroom. She'd arrived late intentionally to avoid the receiving line. Now the floor was thronged with costumed guests—mermaids shook their satin tails at Indian chiefs, Cleopatras and high school drum majorettes did the lambada with Zorros and Arab sheiks. It reminded Randy of a lavish Hollywood set, an extravaganza that would have done Cecil B. De Mille proud.

She saw no sign of either Santeras or Geoff in the crowd, not that she would have recognized them if they'd been in costume. Her own vivid turquoise harem outfit was modest compared to some of the erotic feathered and jeweled creations the women were wearing. She'd been uneasy about the voluptuous way her breasts spilled from the sequined, strapless bra and the sheerness of her low-slung harem pants. It had even occurred to her in the taxi that the only thing people couldn't see was her face!

She checked to make sure her veil was securely attached as she joined the festive celebration. Lights sparkled and flashed from crystal chandeliers, and a Latin orchestra played against a waterfall backdrop of shimmering gold lamé. Someone brought her a drink of something that bubbled like champagne but tasted like peaches. Randy had to lift her veil to sip it.

In the next room, she found table after table groaning with platters of gourmet delights, every kind of delicacy imaginable. She avoided the marinated raw squid, but tried a scoop of pink salmon mousse on a pitch-black cracker and found it delicious.

Continuing her tour, she wandered out onto a moon-drenched veranda where flamenco guitarists drifted among the guests, serenading amorous couples. Several stag males looked her over, their provocative smiles making her wonder whether they were interested in dancing or something more intimate. She smiled at the prospect. And to think, if she'd listened to Geoff Dias, she would have missed all this.

There was still no sign of Carlos Santeras as she moved from room to room, exploring the villa. She hadn't spotted Geoff either, though she'd expected his size would give him away. It was ridiculously easy to be anonymous at a huge costume ball, she realized.

Encouraged to try some serious investigating, she searched for a stairway to take her to the lower floor. A small bank of elevators stood in a hallway off one of the dining rooms, but Randy didn't like the looks of the guard posted nearby. Even if his black tights hadn't discouraged her, his executioner's hood would have.

Realizing a minor diversion was in order, she began to search for a smoke alarm and found one near the kitchen. She set it off with a nail file from her purse, a trick she'd learned in the apartment project where she grew up. She hid in a guest bathroom as several guards rushed by.

The elevators were clear when she got back to them. She stepped inside and pressed the button to the lower floor, then waited for the doors to close. Her heart sped up as if trying to compensate for the doors' excruciating slowness. It was only a matter of seconds, but that was all it took to convince her how truly vulnerable she was.

The lower floor was dimly lit and frankly ominous. Randy cautiously surveyed the area before stepping out of the elevator. She didn't see any guards, but there was no point in taking any chances. The main corridor, lit only by wall sconces, branched off into a maze of narrow arteries.

There were several locked vaultlike doors on the first corridor she tried, causing her to wonder if they might be temperature-controlled storage rooms for the price-less art Santeras was said to have smuggled in his gangster days.

The doors on the next corridor were painted with a dull black finish and looked as if they might house tiny, dungeonlike cells. The first one Randy tried was un-locked, and to her surprise, it was a small, lavishly appointed apartment with a canopied bed in red satin. Mirrors lined the bed's roof and silky black cords hung from each bedpost. Hardly your typical guest room, she thought, wondering what she'd stumbled into.

A faint sound caught her attention as she was closing the door. She hesitated, listening, and heard it again. The metallic whir of elevator doors. Someone else was on the floor! She doubted that she'd been followed, but she didn't want to be caught by Santeras or one of his guards.

She set off down the corridor, heading for a red door at the end, which she prayed was some kind of an exit. She was breathless by the time she'd covered the short dis-tance, mostly from fear. The knob turned when she tried it, to her great relief. But the door wasn't an exit. It opened onto a large room, dimly lit by more wall sconces.

Randy entered cautiously, closing the door behind her. As her eyes adjusted to the darkness, she could discern rich tapestries hanging on the walls and some bizarre antique equipment. Like the ballroom upstairs, this room made her think of an elaborate movie set. But more than anything, it resembled a medieval torture chamber. There was a wooden structure that might have been a rack and another that looked like a pillory. Along one wall, ropes hung from the ceiling with leather cuffs attached as restraints.

Randy's heart was pounding, but she was more fascinated than frightened. She approached a display of iron masks, struck by their mournful expressions. As she reached to touch one, the door creaked behind her. The sound hit her like an electric shock, paralyzing her for an instant. Before she could turn, two massive arms had encased her and lifted her off the ground.

"No!" She screamed and kicked wildly, but her captor was a burly giant of a man. He carried her across the room as if she were an unruly child, subduing her struggles easily as he brought her arms above her head and secured her wrists in the leather cuffs that were suspended from the ceiling.

"What are you doing?" she gasped as he manacled her ankles too. His black executioner's hood told her he was one of the guards, but he wouldn't speak or respond to her in any way as he fastened the buckles on the ankle restraints. As soon as he'd finished, he rose and left the room.

"Wait!" Randy cried. Fear engulfed her as she struggled against the cuffs and realized she couldn't break free. She screamed for help, knowing no one could hear her with the noise of the party on the floor above. But she had to do something! She'd never been able to deal with constraints of any kind. They threw her into a panic.

She was trying to work one of her hands through the cuff when the guard returned moments later. He was followed by a man who wore monk's robes, his face shadowed by a dark, voluminous hood. The two men spoke in hushed Portuguese, and then the guard walked to Randy and removed what was left of her veil, exposing her features.

"So you came to my party," the man in robes said. "I thought you might."

Randy still couldn't make out the man's face, but she did recognize his voice. It was Carlos Santeras. "Let me go," she said. "Please! I haven't done anything."

"There's nothing to fear," he assured her. "I only want to ask you some questions."

"Questions about what?"

"Your fiancé, Hugh Hargrove. Actually, I have just one question, Ms. Witherspoon. Where is he?"

"I don't know! Really, I don't. Hugh's been missing for days. That's why I came here—"

"You thought you'd find him here? Why?"

Randy didn't see any point in holding back what little she knew. "He was last seen with you," she said.

Santeras drew back the monk's hood, his dark eyes flaring with icy passion. "Your fiancé has made a fatal mistake, Ms. Witherspoon. First he lied to me, and then he tried to bribe me as if I were a common criminal, the kind of scum that attacked you on the street today. He insulted my name, defamed me."

"Bribery? No—" Randy tried to tell him that it must have been a mistake, but he cut her off.

"You can't defend him," he said harshly. "A man must do that for himself. It's a matter of honor."

"Then please, let me go!" Randy strained against the cuffs. "I'll find Hugh, I'll talk to him. If he did what you say, there must be something he can do to make amends."

Santeras studied her, his eyes going cold. "Stop wasting my time, Ms. Witherspoon. Tell me where he is."

"I don't know."

"In that case let me give you a little history lesson, shall I?" He kicked the iron chain attached to her ankle cuffs. "The leather jewelry you're wearing was used to restrain slaves in the days when this villa was a coffee plantation. It proved to be a very effective means of punishment. That's why I hope you're telling the truth."

"I am!"

"Perhaps," he said, "but I have to be sure." He stepped back and replaced his hood. With a quick nod to the guard, he left the room.

Randy let out a terrified moan as she realized what was happening. The guard's eyes glittered, their obvious excitement made more horrible by the executioner's hood. He looked Randy up and down, slowly, lasciviously, and then he began to circle her, making remarks in Portuguese that needed no interpretation.

He stroked her bare skin with his fingers, dragging them along the small of her back and onto her midriff as he came around to face her. Randy shuddered and tried to wrench away from him, but the restraints bit into her flesh.

"Call Mr. Santeras back!" she insisted. "I'm telling the truth, I swear!"

Laughing at her efforts to defend herself, the guard drew a knife from a sheath beneath his shirt. His eyes glowed with a terrible light as he traced the swell of her cleavage with the knife's tip, leaving a thin pink line of enflamed skin. As she flinched back, he slipped the flashing blade under the center band of her bra and severed the material.

Randy screamed in terror as the bra flew open, baring her breasts. The guard snorted with satisfaction, devouring her with his eyes. As he reached out to touch her Randy turned her head away, as repulsed by the sight of him as she was by the thought of his hands on her body.

She waited, skin crawling, for his touch. Instead, she heard a grunt of surprise and looked up to see the guard jerked off his feet and flung against the wall. Geoff had come up on the man from behind! Randy went limp with relief.

The guard never had a chance to recover. As he staggered away from the wall Geoff fell upon him with the jealous passion of a lover fending off a rival. Geoff's fury was awesome. He shook the man until his teeth rattled, threatening to kill him, then knocked him out with one skull-shattering blow.

Randy strained against the cuffs, desperate to be free as she waited for Geoff to bind and gag the unconscious guard. When he was done with the man, he dragged him to a closet and locked him inside.

"Untie me," she pleaded as Geoff turned to her. But her heart froze as she saw the heat burning in his eyes. He believed she'd deceived him, and he was furious.

"Geoff, please," she implored.

He studied her, still breathing hard as he took in her naked breasts and what was left of her harem outfit. Randy felt a sharp thrill of alarm. He looked as if he intended to take up where the guard had left off.

"What's wrong with you?" she cried. "Untie me! We have to get out of here!"

"What's the rush?" His voice was dangerously soft. "Santeras won't be back tonight. He's got a party to host. That's why he left you in the hands of his thug rather than 'interrogate' you himself."

"Dammit, Geoff, you have to let me go! Santeras is after Hugh, and he thinks I know where Hugh is."

"Maybe you should have thought of that before you came to this party, sweetness. I seem to remember suggesting that possibility."

Geoff wiped the back of his hand across his forehead, sweeping waves of damp hair from his eyes. A nerve sparked painfully in his jaw, triggered by the adrenaline still coursing through him. He knew she was frantic to be set free, but he had no intention of untying her, no intention in hell. She was too wildly erotic with her bared breasts and her anguished sighs. And he was too aroused and angry and frustrated to give in to his nobler instincts at that moment.

"How did you find me?" she asked, as if hoping to distract him.

"I heard your screams." Anger flashed as he remembered how badly she'd frightened him. He'd had no idea she was in danger, or even that she'd come to the party, until he'd followed Santeras and his guard to this floor. He'd lost track of them in the maze of corridors when he'd heard a woman's shriek. He'd known instinctively that it was Randy, and his heart had nearly slammed through his chest.

"I could scream again," she threatened.

"Go right ahead, but it's you they'll find. And don't expect me to come riding to the rescue."

She swore at him and twisted against her bonds, but he made no move in her direction. He was fighting a dozen different impulses, the most immediate of which was to stay exactly where he was and let her beg for a while. He wanted her to throb wondering what he was going to do—and waiting for him to do it.

He let his eyes run the length of her body, trying to imagine how in hell he ever got mixed up with a heartbreaker like her. Her back was arched defiantly, and her skin was flushed with heat, glowing from her throat to her breasts. The sight of her enflamed him.

"Geoff!"

"Don't go anywhere," he said, letting the darkness he felt roughen his voice. He walked to the door, locked and bolted it, then turned back to her.

Randy waited, agonized, sensing what he intended. She moaned softly as he approached, her mind on fire. The idea of him touching her while she was restrained whipped her into a fever pitch of excitement. "You can't," she whispered.

"Can't what?" he asked.

The anticipation she felt was nearly unbearable as he walked up to her. With his hair falling all around him in crazy disarray and his eyes as piercing as emerald shards, he looked capable of anything. She told herself not to move, knowing every breath that rushed through her lungs made her belly tighten and her breasts shake. She knew how she must look, stretched out and trembling, like a nubile slave restrained for her master's pleasure.

"Please," she said, "don't . . . touch me."

The muscles of his jaw went taut. "You're reading my mind, sweetness."

"You wouldn't," she said, ashamed of her own desperation—and hating him for making her that way. "You wouldn't take advantage, not like this. You're not that kind of man."

"Oh, that's rich." He laughed harshly. "I've been

called everything from a bastard to a barbarian, but suddenly I'm not that kind of man." His gaze dropped to her breasts, and he blew a soft jet of air over her cleavage, cooling the perspiration that had beaded there. "What kind of man am I, Randy? Why don't you tell me, since you seem to be the expert?"

"You're a monster!" A sob thickened her voice. "And I *hate* you."

Laughing he continued to cool her down, purling air over her throat, her lips. "Now we're getting somewhere," he said. "Tell me how much you hate me, Randy. Tell my *why* you hate me."

"Because you're crude and uncouth—" She hesitated as if trying to think of something else. "And you ride a motorcycle."

"Sure, sure, but why do you really hate me?"

She flushed a deep red. "Because of the way you look at me, the way you talk to me. You make me feel . . . dirty."

"Dirty!" He howled at the word. "You should be thanking me for that. Has Hugh ever made you feel dirty?"

"Of course not! Hugh treats me like a lady."

"Yeah, I'll just bet he does. I'll bet Prince Charming kisses you all nice and neat and doesn't even mess up your hair. I'll bet Hugh's a fastidious lover, isn't he? In at ten, out at ten-fifteen? Simultaneous climaxes? All nice and tidy?"

"You're *disgusting!*"

His breath shook as he studied her. "And you like it, don't you?" He began to walk around her, circling her slowly, lowering his voice to a husky murmur. "If you know anything about me at all, Randy, you know I'd never treat you like a lady. I'd treat you like a woman. I'd mess you up a little, and I'd keep you that way— messy, sexy, wet—just for me."

Randy reared up in shock. She breathed in sharply, and then she went weak against the restraints, her legs refusing to hold her. A powerful current of excitement was flowing through her, making her tremble, and yet deep inside, there was the wildest, sweetest ache, seizing up and clutching at her muscles. If she hadn't been bound, she would have sagged to the floor.

"*Stop it*," she said, fighting for strength. She twisted away from the cooling air that bathed her shoulders and breasts, refusing to look at him, refusing to participate in any more of his outrageous games. "Don't talk to me anymore," she said, her voice shaking.

She felt the pull of his silence, but she didn't look up.

"Why not?" he asked finally. "Are you afraid of what I'm going to say, of how it might make you feel? I don't even have to touch you, do I, baby? I can just talk to you and you get hot."

"Please," she breathed. "Don't!" She could feel a kind of shuddering in her depths. It was strange and potent and beautiful, as if she were coming apart. It made her want to draw up, to protect herself, but she couldn't with her legs restrained. She was helpless against the feelings. Her breasts were throbbing with excitement. Her thighs ached softly. He did make her feel like a woman. But he made her feel those other things too, totally unacceptable things! Sexy and dirty. Why was that so thrilling?

"Don't do this," she said urgently. "You're torturing me."

"I'm not even touching you, Randy."

Geoff was well aware of her anguish, but he couldn't stop himself. The sight of her half-naked and flushed with turmoil fed into his more primitive male needs. The restraints against her pale skin made her seem delicate, vulnerable. But even if he'd wanted to free her, he couldn't have done it at that moment. He'd waited too long for this. He wanted to feel her naked breasts trembling under his touch. He wanted to make her heart rip out of control, just as his had.

He wanted some satisfaction.

She shuddered as he moved closer, close enough to tilt her head up and kiss her, close enough to cup her breasts.

Something near agony moved in her eyes as she looked up at him. "Why are you doing this to me?"

"Maybe I have to." His breathing went odd and harsh as he fought the need to give in to her, to end her torment. "Maybe I want to hear you admit it."

"Admit what?"

"That you liked it, Randy. That you liked it with me, that you'd like it again."

She moaned and swayed, almost sensually. It aroused the hell out of him hearing the sounds she made, watching her twist against the restraints. Her breasts shivered and swung with her movements, and her skin was flushed with heat. But it was her nipples that made his groin ache like fire. They were drawn, beautifully taut. They reminded him of how hard he was, how badly he wanted to make love to her.

"You're beautiful, Randy," he admitted huskily. "I want you. *I do want you.*"

Randy went still at his admission, shuddering inside, waiting for his touch. Every cell in her body was waiting, every nerve. She closed her eyes, sighing, quaking. Wanting it . . . *yes*, wanting it. But he didn't touch her. His fingers never found her. His hands never claimed her breasts, easing their pain. Instead, he began to move around her again, arousing her with words, telling her with soft, searing heat what he would do to her if he were her lover.

She sagged against the restraints, unable to stand. The quaking inside her was terrible, beautiful. It broke over her like a wave, leaving her weak with stimulation, incoherent with need. She closed her eyes and whispered the words he wanted to hear. *Be my lover.*

"What, baby? I can't hear you."

He was going to make her say it again!

"Be my lover," she pleaded, opening her eyes.

Pain flared through his features as he came to stand before her. He cupped her breast, searing her to her soul. "You already have a lover," he said. "Who do you want? Me or Hugh?"

Randy shook her head frantically. She wanted *him*, even though she knew it meant giving up everything, her dream, her fairy-tale future. "You," she whispered. A moan ripped through her as he bent and took her breast in his mouth, drowning her flesh in fire. "I want you!"

But even as she uttered the words, she knew she couldn't go through with them. The instant they were out of her mouth, she began to shake her head and cry. "No, I can't," she gasped, flinching away from him, begging him to understand. "I can't!"

Something snapped inside her then. Something went crazy in the dark recesses of her mind. "Stop!" she cried. He tried to keep her from flailing, but she twisted away from his hands. She was still fighting him, still writhing and crying when she realized that he'd cut her free from the leather restraints. She dropped into his arms, faint with sexual heat, torn by emotion and confusion.

Geoff gathered her in his arms, his heart pounding wildly. He wanted her with a ferocity that frightened him. And he could easily have taken advantage of the situation. She didn't have the strength to resist him, and she was as aroused as he was. But he didn't want her that way, confused about what she was doing, why she was doing it—and especially *who* she was doing it with.

He was also aware that he'd endangered their safety by delaying their escape. Despite what he'd told her about Santeras being occupied, he knew the man could show up at any time.

"Can you stand up?" he asked Randy, stripping off his shirt and wrapping it around her.

She nodded, still dazed, groggy.

"Come on," he said gently, drawing her into his arms and soothing her until she stopped shuddering. "I know another way out of this dive. I've been here before." She leaned into him heavily, letting him support her weight as they started for the door.

Eleven

Geoff's other way out of the villa involved an air-conditioning shaft and a claustrophobic climb to the surface. They escaped onto the grounds through an air-intake vent and then found the bike where Geoff had parked it, in a concealing thicket of banyan trees. It was a harrowing ordeal, but it took Randy's mind off the tangle of nerves inside her, and it got them out of the villa without being spotted.

She barely had the strength to hold on to Geoff as they sped toward the entrance gates of the grounds on his motorcycle moments later. She was too dazed to worry about whether or not the guard would let them out. But apparently Geoff had some kind of "understanding" with the man, and the next thing she knew, they were zigzagging along the serpentine road that descended the mountain.

She pressed herself to Geoff, nestling her face into the valley of his shoulders as they caromed through the moist, jungle-scented darkness. All she wanted now was for her body to stop throbbing. And to be safe.

She'd just begun to relax when Geoff pulled the bike into the driveway of a cliffside bungalow that overlooked the glimmering harbor lights of Botafogo Bay.

"This is a friend's place," he explained. "We can't go back to the hotel tonight. Santeras might look for you there."

Randy found the wood-shake bungalow charming with its bougainvillea-wreathed arbors and breathtaking view. "Whose house is it?" she asked.

Geoff helped her off the bike and dismounted. "It belongs to a former customer, a wealthy American businessman, whose wife and daughter were taken hostage during a military coup in Guatemala. My partners and I got them out."

"Really?" She eyed him with a skeptical smile. "You never mentioned this place while I was haggling with the reservations clerk for a room."

Geoff snagged her hand and brought her along with him as he walked toward the hacienda's entrance. "I wanted to see what you could do, tiger."

If Randy was charmed by the outside of the house, she was enchanted by the inside. Golden wood tones dominated, warming couches done in dusty-rose chintz and maple curios stocked with china. The wall overlooking the bay was a long curve of glass with a breathtaking view that was totally unobstructed, even by the terrace, which was a flight of stairs below.

She stood at the window, hugging Geoff's shirt around her and gazing down at the twinkling necklace of lights that outlined the harbor. She'd seen postcards of a similar view, but none of them had done it justice. It was almost too lovely to take in.

"Do you like the place?" Geoff asked, coming up behind her.

"I love it." She turned to him and saw the anticipation she felt mirrored in his eyes. It was the perfect romantic hideaway. They both knew it.

He touched her arm.

"Geoff, I can't," she said, her voice throaty and low. Longing welled inside her as she shook her head. She couldn't, but she wanted to, *she wanted to.*

"Yes, I know."

The whispered words were harsh with disappointment. They totally surprised her. Did he know? Did he finally understand her conflict? His touch was gone, with no more pressure than a breath of air. It could have been a warm breeze caressing her skin, except that a breeze would never have brought her such a keen sense of loss. *Be my lover*, she thought.

Unable to suppress the longing, she searched his face, perhaps for some kind of reassurance that he might want more than a repeat of the past, more than just one night of sex. She searched her own memory. What kind of man was he? she asked herself. She was as drawn to his harsh beauty now as she had been the night she met him, a mysterious drifter cruising through town.

She knew in her heart that Geoff Dias could never be part of her life. He was too wild and primitive to be the man of her dreams. She could never live the life he'd chosen, and she was sure he could never adjust to hers. What kind of husband could he possibly be, what kind of father? She knew nothing about him really, except that he could be perverse and passionate and was addicted to fast motorcycles. *So why was she standing here, gazing at him, longing for him?*

"What is it?" he asked her. "You're looking at me like a kid with her nose pressed to a store window."

"I can't help myself . . . I want to be with you."

His reaction brought her a quiver of guilty pleasure. He looked confused, thunderstruck. His hand was unsteady as he touched her face.

"Randy?"

"It's true," she said, closing her eyes for a second, nuzzling against the warmth of his fingers. "I'm an engaged woman whose fiancé is missing. I should be thinking about Hugh, nothing but Hugh. But I'm not doing that, Geoff. I'm thinking about other things, bad things, us . . . together."

He said her name again, softly.

She turned away from him and stared out the window, needing to get the rest of it out. "The wanting is terrible. It's a knife inside me, cutting me to pieces. My willpower is gone, my sense of right and wrong. I hardly have anything left holding me together. It's ripping away at everything I thought was important."

She hesitated, shuddering, and took a breath. "It's killing me, this wanting. But I can't give in to it, Geoff, I *can't*."

"Randy, for God's sake!" He turned her around, staring at her, disbelieving.

She swayed with the power he gave off, craving the strength of his hands on her shoulder, loving the firmness of his grip as he anchored her in place. She wanted to fall into his arms so badly. It would be so easy, so thrilling to give in to him.

"I can't do it," she insisted, her voice grainy, aching. "I'm engaged to another man. And even if I wasn't, you don't want the things I want. You don't even want me, except for just one night. I can't do that."

"Why? Because you'd be betraying Hugh, a man you don't even love?"

"I'd be betraying myself. Don't you understand that? Don't you see how important this is to me? I want to be something more than I was. I have to be."

"Why, Randy? What the hell's wrong with who you are?"

Some sweet kind of pain she barely understood welled up inside her. "This is not who I *am*," she said, desperate to make him understand. "I'm the illegitimate brat of a woman who had to work nights as a barmaid to pay the rent. The neighbors snickered and whispered behind our backs, they snubbed my mother to her face! All they cared about was that she had men over, men who gave her a little bit of pleasure, but robbed her of every ounce of self-respect."

"Men who made her feel dirty?" he asked, releasing her.

"Yes"—she sighed the word—"that too."

He stood back from her, silent, as if he didn't like what was going through his mind. "I'm beginning to understand the attraction to Hugh," he said at last.

Randy turned back to the window, struggling to find enough control to talk. The subject of her childhood was private, painful, but there was so much misery stored up inside her, so much that needed to come out.

"When you're a kid . . . and you have a dream," she told him, "sometimes it becomes everything, a way to survive, to get from one day to the next. That's how it was for me. Cinderella and the prince. Ridiculous, huh?"

"Maybe not," he said.

Randy felt a sharp tug at her heart. There was something near compassion in his voice, and she would never have expected that from him, not in her case. Was he acknowledging the things she'd told him? Was he beginning to understand? She turned back to him and wanted to cry, he looked so grave, so beautifully sad. She still wanted him. God, she did.

"We all have dreams, Randy."

"It's just that I'm so close," she told him pleadingly. "So close to having mine. Don't ruin it, Geoff. *Don't ruin me.* You could . . . so easily."

He let out a sound that was too harsh to be laughter. "Never let it be said that Geoff Dias stood between the lady and her dream."

She could see the emotion he was fighting, and it nearly destroyed her. Rather than cry in front of him, she fled the room.

Geoff didn't try to stop her. He didn't trust himself to say anything, do anything at that moment. The muscles of his throat had drawn up like catgut, and it was all he could do to swallow. From somewhere in the house the silvery chimes of a clock rang out. The sound was ethereal, lonely. It sharpened the emptiness rather than filled it.

She wants the dream, Dias. Get used to it.

A collection of crystal decanters crowded a lacquered tray on the wet bar, and Geoff wasted no time pouring himself a generous amount of one-hundred-proof rum. He drank it straight and grimaced at the oily afterburn. Anything to fill the void, he thought. Anything to kill the pain. Whatever works. For her it was success, the American dream. That had stopping working for him a long time ago.

Hell, if he had a dream these days, it was simple survival—cheating death, staying alive long enough to draw his next breath. Nothing too complicated.

Not that he hadn't tried it all—sex, booze, rock and roll. He and his two partners in recovery operations had been made heroes by the media for some of their exploits, and he'd been tagged the "bad boy" of the bunch. The publicity had come in handy later when he was setting up Stealth International, but it had taken the challenge out of his love life. Women were willing to do just about anything for—and with—a national hero. Even the sex got boring after awhile . . . until her.

Survival, Dias. Don't think about her.

He splashed more rum into the tumbler, unheeding as some of it spilled over the side, and then he walked to the glass terrace doors. The panel slid open soundlessly, sultry warmth rushing in. Raking his hair back off his forehead, Geoff let the steambath of a night envelop him. It felt good, it felt hot . . . it felt like her.

Aw hell, he thought, a shudder running through him.

Don't do this, man. Survival—

He stared down at the bay, clutching the slippery glass in his hand, shaking his head back and forth slowly. Trouble, dammit. He was in trouble. He had a strange feeling shifting in the pit of his gut, and he felt cold suddenly, dampness filming his forehead. At first he thought there was something wrong with the rum.

And then he knew it wasn't rum making him sweat. It wasn't heat or a tropical bug or anything like that.

It was her. It was this damned mission they were on. He was about to find her fiancé for her and then hand her over to the yuppie bastard! Best wishes, kids! Have a nice marriage and maybe a couple of precocious little brats with horn-rimmed glasses and button-down collars like Hugh. Just the thought of it made him sweat. It made him sick.

He stared at the glass clenched in his hand, at the rigid tension in his bloodless fingers.

Aw hell . . . holy hell, he was in trouble.

There's no surviving this one, Dias. You're dead, man. You're in love.

He finished off the rum in one gulp and flung the glass into the bay, then he strode back into the house for the bottle.

Love? Jesus! He wasn't on intimate terms with that particular emotion. He wasn't even friendly with it. He'd seen what love could do, even the sweetest, most devoted kind of love. His father had committed suicide when Geoff was a teenager, and his mother, unable to bear the loss, had overdosed on sleeping pills shortly after. It was called accidental, but Geoff knew she hadn't wanted to live. She'd adored his father. Geoff had adored them both. His life had never been the same after that.

"Geoff . . . ?"

He was about to take a swig from the fifth of rum when he heard her whisper his name. He set the bottle down and turned to the most incredible sight he'd ever seen. Randy was standing in the hall doorway, her nude body bathed in moonlight.

"What are you doing?" he asked.

She wet her lips, looking helpless, irresistible.

"Randy, what—? Why are you doing this?"

"Don't ask me why," she said, her voice shaking. "All I know is I need to be with you."

Geoff's heart went dangerously weak. What was she saying? That she wanted him over Hugh, that she'd chosen him? Her eyes said she needed him urgently, but he knew it had gone beyond the point of casual sex for both of them. He couldn't make love to her and let her go. He shook his head, not wanting this to happen, yet wanting her so badly it was painful.

"Randy, don't do this unless you're sure . . ." He let the sentence trail off, mesmerized by her dazzling, anguished smile and the tears welling in her eyes.

Survival, Dias . . .

But the warning went unheeded as she held out her hand to him. He didn't even remember going over to her, but he must have, because a moment later they were hand in hand, walking slowly toward the bungalow's bedroom. He knew she must be feeling the same disorientation, the same crazy magic he was. They were moving as though in a daze, both of them, a dream all of their own, not willing to speak or even to think, not willing to let anything intrude.

She touched his face as they reached the bedroom, a tremor in her fingers, and Geoff felt himself hardening. The energy slamming through his groin brought him so much pleasure, he wanted to groan. A touch and he was gone. One innocent touch! He thought immediately of the other time she'd aroused him and sent him over the edge. But he couldn't let her do that to him this time. He needed to be in control.

Her hand fluttered down his neck to his chest, a gypsy bride trying to steal his heart, his soul. She started to tug at his T-shirt, but he stopped her, capturing her hand in the hollow of his breastbone, pressing it against the riot of excitement inside him.

The room streamed with moonlight. It shimmered silver through her ebony hair and caught the sparkle of emotion in her eyes. Fear or desire? He couldn't tell. But her body seemed to glow with anticipation, her breasts and hipbones shivering, iridescent.

"How come I'm the only one naked?" she asked shakily.

"Because I want it that way," he told her.

"Why? Aren't we going to—"

"Oh, yes," he promised roughly, imprisoning her hand as he reached down to unzip his pants. "We're going to. We're going to rock this house. We're going to rock Rio. You and I are going to be sexier than Carnaval, hotter and sweeter than *cachaça*."

"Then why can't I undress you?"

He couldn't believe she didn't know. She couldn't be that innocent. She had to be aware of the effect she had on him. He was a hopeless case, reduced to animal instincts by the sound of her voice, the willful tilt of her chin, the hot little flare of her nostrils. One touch of her hand and he was gone.

Maybe a little object lesson was in order, he decided.

He reached in and freed himself from the confines of his fly, shuddering at the feel of so much energy springing free. He was all heat and muscle—one hardened, rampant muscle.

"Because of this," he said, guiding her hand to his groin. Her fingers fluttered over him so exquisitely, he had to pull them away. But her gasp brought him soaring pleasure.

"Now do you see why I want you naked?" he said, kissing the same fingertips that had just driven him wild, rubbing them against his lips. "I want the edge this time, baby. I want some control."

"No—you want *me* out of control, crazy for you . . ." Her voice softened on a throaty groan, and she barely got the next words out. ". . . wet for you."

He kissed her knuckles, inadvertently biting down on them as his desire became pain. "This is survival, Randy. I've got so much feeling raging inside me, It could kill me if I let it."

She looked up at him, her eyes going liquid, the dark irises melting into pools of heat. "Let it, Geoff," she said softly, wetting her lips with her tongue, seducing him with her urgent, husky voice. "Let it kill you, just a little."

She touched him with her free hand, stroking him before he could stop her. "Let me," she murmured, bending as if to take him into her mouth.

He seized her by the arms and brought her back up. "No way, sweetness," he said huskily. "You're not getting near that stick of dynamite. We'd both explode." He lifted her to him and kissed her, caressing her lips lightly, tautly, controlling the tripwire tension he felt. "Now stand up, Randy," he murmured, "like a good girl. And open your legs."

"Me?"

"Yes, you. Definitely you."

"Like this? Standing up?"

"Just like this."

Randy breathed out a shivering sound as she stared into his eyes. He was asking her to do something unspeakably erotic, and surrendering that much control to him frightened her. Anxiety leaped inside her as she realized how vulnerable she would be, how exposed.

"Do it, baby," he said gently.

She moved her legs apart, and a soft moan slipped from her lips as he stepped back to look at her. His gaze drifted from her swollen breasts to the juncture of her thighs, and Randy felt herself beginning to shudder, to ache inside. Impelled by some forbidden impulse, she moved her legs wider and waited for that touch, that deeper, incredibly private touch.

His exhalation was the only sound in the room.

It seemed a lifetime before he came to stand before her. And even then he surprised her, startling a moan out of her as he ran his hands slowly up her naked thighs. It wasn't what she expected, any more than she expected him to cup her buttocks and stare into her eyes. "I've got this terrible thirst," he said at last, bending to take her breast into his mouth. His lips pulled irresistibly at her nipple, sipping and tugging, drinking her in. Randy arched against him, her legs spread wide, her sharp moans mingling with his.

He left her breasts sweetly aching and purled down her body with the soft friction of sand-washed silk. She tightened instinctively as he trailed kisses over her belly and down each thigh, avoiding the heartbeat of her need, the place where she throbbed for him. And just when she thought he would never touch her there, never kiss her there, he did.

"Oh, God," she breathed as he pressed his lips into the curly dark hair that crowned her thighs. A hot flush of awareness spread through her as he began to discover her secrets with his lips and his tongue. Her stomach clutched with the raw, sweet pleasure of it, and she moved against him, rhythmically, wantonly, forgetting to be ashamed.

She gasped tightly, arching up when he came upon the place where her nerves were thrumming with electricity. It was the most intense pleasure she'd ever known. It was glorious, soaring toward a peak, but never going over, hovering, hovering.

"You're sweet, Randy," he said, bracing her thighs with his hands. "Sweeter than *cachaça*."

But Randy couldn't respond. She was too stunned, too overcome with stimulation. Every sense was heightened. She could feel his golden mane of hair caressing her skin, tickling her nerves, and his tongue sliding against the very center of her being. She could feel it all at once, rushing at her like a sensory storm, and her body didn't know how to respond. Her legs were vibrating wildly, unable to hold her up.

"Geoff, *please*," she groaned.

She sagged against him, tangling her hands in his hair, crazy for things she couldn't bring herself to verbalize. She felt him shudder and reach for her, pulling her down to the floor with him. She thought he was going to make love to her right there, but the next thing she knew, he was lifting her in his arms, carrying her to the bed, kissing her, lowering his weight onto her.

She was already climaxing wildly when he entered her.

Geoff pulled her into his arms and hugged her tightly. He was fighting to hold back his own release as he penetrated her trembling body, thrusting deeply and uncontrollably that first time, that first enflamed time.

"Randy, sweetness," he murmured, astonished at the way her cries cut through him, at the way her muscles clutched at him. He'd had sex more times than he could count, and with more women than he cared to remember, but everything he'd come to know and believe about the experience was negated the moment he impaled himself in her tender, pulsing flesh. He felt like a virgin. He *was* a virgin. He'd never had sex before, not with a woman he loved. Jesus, the thought of it staggered him.

Her eyes were wet with tears as she looked up at him, her chin trembling uncontrollably. "I need to feel you, Geoff, please. I need you naked everywhere, inside me, against me."

She caught hold of his shoulders, piercing him with her fingernails as she tried to pull off his T-shirt. She was wet and messy and beautiful, every inch the sad, proud gypsy he remembered.

"I'll do it," he said, withdrawing long enough to rip off his shirt and kick his pants free. When he reentered her, she began to climax again, inciting him to wild heights of passion. A surge of longing shook through him as he kissed her and rolled with her, pulling her on top of him, plunging deeply inside her body. He took her with all the sweet, crazy abandon of their first night together, and yet there was a bursting tenderness in the way he arched into her flesh this time, tenderness in the way he held her.

Before it was over, he was as naked as she was, emotionally and physically. He had completely surrendered to the power, to the miracle of their joined flesh. His body throbbed, bringing him to a climax that shook his soul. His feelings for her ran deep and torrential, a spring flood that took out everything in its path.

In the last throes, he wondered if he would survive it. His mind answered him as he collapsed into Randy's arms, gathering her up, being gathered up, holding and being held, everything joined, everything one, their breath, their bodies. . . .

You're dead, Dias. You're in love.

Randy awoke to a sweltering darkness, to a room drenched with heavy sweetness. A wet, steamy breeze oozed through the bedroom's slatted windows, bringing with it the lush perfume of overripe flowers and the briny pungence of salt tides. It was raining outside, she realized, one of the tropical downpours Rio was known for. She glanced down at the man sleeping beside her, a light film of perspiration sheening his nakedness. He lay on his back, one arm thrown out, strong and beautiful in the moonlight, yet oddly vulnerable.

The dampness that cooled her breasts brought her a feverish chill. She felt dizzy and dehydrated—and very sore in several vulnerable places. As she gazed at Geoff, a sigh stirred in her depths, making her want to smile sadly. The irony of the situation struck her. She'd awakened only one other time in bed with a strange man—or in bed with any man, for that matter. It was Geoff Dias then too.

She'd run away that night. This night she had to do something much more painful. She had to decide. She pulled the sheets around her, shivering in the damp heat as that prospect tore at her. She had always imagined when she found the right man, she would fall madly in love and be caught up in the sweeping passion that came with wedding vows and happily-ever-afters. That vision had built a longing within her that Hugh had never been able to fulfill.

Another irony struck her as she studied Geoff's golden hair, his rugged, sunburned features. He was that man, she realized. Geoff Dias was her dream lover, the one who could fulfill her sexually and perhaps even emotionally in a way that Hugh never could. Geoff was the dream. But only Hugh could *give* her the dream. Hugh was stable and successful, socially accomplished, the perfect man, the perfect husband. Marrying him would prove as nothing else could that she had escaped the past and the curse that destroyed her mother.

She knew all that, but it didn't ease her turmoil any.

She rose from the bed and picked up the cotton bedspread from the floor where it had dropped, wrapping it around her. Geoff stirred, and as she turned to look at him she realized how badly she wanted to return to the warmth of his arms. It was a hook that tugged at her vitals, ripped at her. Surely he could ward off the sadness and protect her from the pain. Surely his strength could keep the demons at bay.

But for how long?

She couldn't avoid the fears that were creeping into her awareness, the damning questions. How long would it take before he grew restless? How long before he grew bored and moved on, the way all Edna's men had?

Some time later she found herself in the living room, staring out the window at the rain. It had lightened to a steamy mist, and the glimmering harbor lanterns were visible again, Sugarloaf outlined against a moonlit horizon.

If Geoff Dias had been sent to test her commitment to Hugh, then she had failed the test. Her turbulent encounter with him had shaken every belief she had, every certainty. It was forcing her to look at herself, to examine her choices. And yet what choices did he present? What options did he bring to her life?

Would he even want to be a part of her life?

She had no idea how long she stood there, searching her heart for answers that could only bring her more pain. But as dawn began to break, she could feel an easing of the turmoil inside her, a coherence beginning to take shape in her thoughts. And finally daylight swelled, bringing with it her sanity, her salvation. This was her day of reckoning, she realized, and finally she knew what had to be done, knew it with a certainty that burned away her confusion and brought her the momentary relief that came with having made a choice.

She touched the window as the pain hit her.

Geoff roused and rolled to his side, his body aching in every joint. He felt as if he'd been ten rounds in the ring with a world-class opponent. The thought made him smile. She was that, he admitted. Easily world-class.

With a husky groan he sat up and looked around the room. "Randy?" the other side of the bed was empty, but her harem pants and bra lay on the floor where she'd discarded them last night before she'd appeared in the living room, naked.

Deep muscles tightened at that memory, and Geoff winced as if he'd pulled something. At thirty-seven he was probably in the best condition of his life, but he'd used some new muscles last night. Or maybe he'd used the old ones in new ways.

"Randy?"

He rolled off the bed and stood, combing a hand through his hair as he tried to smooth out some of the tangles. A glance in the dresser mirror told him he looked like a wild man, a naked wild man. From Borneo maybe. Or Sunset Strip.

He hesitated, rubbing the stubble that shadowed his chin and wondering if he should shave. The rest of his body would pass inspection, he decided, checking out the muscularity of his chest and stomach. He looked fit enough. But had he put on a little extra weight around his waist?

A grimace crossed his face as he realized what he'd been doing. He was checking himself out for flaws. Was this what happened when you fell for a woman? Did you start staring at yourself in mirrors, wondering how you looked to her, wondering if she was going to like what she saw?

He looked around for something to put on and found his fatigue pants lying in a heap near the foot of the bed. As he pulled them on and zipped the fly, last night's passion screened through his mind again. He had some heavy thinking to do, about love and meaningful relationships and what the hell all that meant. But that could wait. In the meantime he just wanted to see her again, maybe kiss her good morning and watch her eat some of his famous chorizo and scrambled eggs. Nothing too strenuous.

There was no sign of her in the living room or the kitchen. But as he wandered through the house, increasingly concerned, he heard murmurs coming from down a hallway where the guest bedroom was located. He stopped at the door and listened. It sounded as if she was in there, talking to someone. His heart froze for an instant. Santeras? Had he found her?

Geoff nudged the door with his foot. His body was spring-tight, ready to fly into action. As he continued to inch the door open, Randy came into his field of vision. She was sitting on the bed, talking on the telephone, tears rolling down her cheeks.

He swung the door open wide, and she looked up. She was alone in the room, and the anguish swimming in her dark eyes told him everything he needed to know.

"It's Hugh," she said, holding her hand over the receiver. "He's alive."

Geoff felt as if he'd been kicked hard in the solar plexus. "That's him on the line? Where is he?"

"No, it's the hospital—" Randy broke off to complete the call. She copied down some information, then mumbled a hurried thank you and hung up the phone.

"What happened?" Geoff asked. He didn't want to know, but he *had* to know. It was the same sick curiosity that made people crane their necks to look at a horrible accident.

She ducked her head, wiping her damp cheeks against the bedspread she was wrapped in. "I called my assistant to tell her where I was," she said, "and she told me they'd been contacted by a doctor in Caracas. Hugh's at a hospital in Venezuela. Somehow he got as far as São Paulo, and from there he chartered a small plane." She swallowed with some effort. "They crashed in the jungle. The pilot was killed, and Hugh was found unconscious. Apparently he'd tried to go for help. He was several miles from the plane, but they say he's going to be all right."

"How about you? Are you all right?" It wasn't the question he wanted to ask. He wanted to know how she felt about him, about them.

"I'm—I don't know . . . in shock, I guess."

He exhaled heavily. "What do you do now?" He didn't need to ask. He knew, he *knew*.

She began to talk quickly, not looking at him. "I've got a flight out this morning, so I suppose I should call a cab and stop at a store to get something to wear. It's probably better that I don't go back to the hotel in case Santeras or his men are there. I can have my things sent home, of course—"

He knew she was trying to postpone the inevitable, but he had to stop her. He had to get it over with. "Just answer one question for me," he said. "Are you going to marry Hugh?"

She nodded and the tears began to flow. "Yes."

The wrench at his heart was deep, brutal. "Then call

that cab and get out of here." He was amazed at the fatalistic tone of his voice, amazed that he wasn't busting up the room. "Go, Randy. Now, while I'm still halfway civilized. Get out of here."

Her chin trembled on a choked sob. "Geoff . . . I'm sorry."

He turned his back, unwilling to let her see the savage contraction of his jaw.

"Please," she said, "please understand that I have to do this. It's my life. It's everything."

In a crazy way he did understand. Even with the pain locking his throat, strangling him, he understood. He could never be what she wanted. He was the wrong man for her, but not for the reasons she thought. No, it wasn't nearly as simple as the fact that he was a biker and she wanted a prince.

"You've got nothing to be sorry for," he told her, echoing the words of another night. "Just go. *Please go.*"

Twelve

"Miranda? Are you all right?"

Hugh Hargrove asked the question from his hospital bed. Peering intently at Randy through his rounded tortoiseshell glasses, he added, "You seem agitated."

Randy winced inwardly at his use of the long form of her name, and then she remembered she'd asked him to call her that some time ago. She'd thought it was more sophisticated than Randy. He'd agreed.

"I'm fine, really," she reassured him, turning away from the window where she'd been distracted by the rainstorm. "I was thinking about our flight home. I hope the weather doesn't get worse."

She forced herself to smile, though he'd been right about the agitation. She was still heartsick, still feeling confused and shaken about the way things had ended with Geoff. "Can I get you anything?" she asked Hugh. "Some water?"

"I'm fine," he insisted, waving her to sit down. "Please, relax."

She turned to the chair, but she couldn't sit. She couldn't relax, and she knew her unrest had nothing to do with Hugh. The doctor had given him a clean bill of health and was discharging him this afternoon. The symptoms of his concussion had cleared, his bacterial infection had responded to medication, and his other injuries were considered minor.

"Hugh," she said, "about the wedding—"

"It's all right. We can postpone it."

"No—" Her throat tightened painfully. "I don't want to postpone it. I want to get married next weekend as we planned. Is that all right?"

He pushed the glasses up on his nose as if to get a closer look at her. "Next weekend?"

She knew he was startled, but she also knew that to delay their wedding would mean letting more fears and doubts creep into her thoughts. She'd never once doubted the rightness of marrying Hugh before Geoff Dias reappeared. Now she had to find that feeling of certainty again, to reclaim her sense of direction, of destiny. She'd told herself that everything would fall into place if they could just follow through with their plans, get their lives back on track.

She walked to his bedside and took his hand. "I want to get home, Hugh, don't you? I want to begin our life together."

"Of course I want that." He squeezed her hand.

"The doctor said you were fine," she reminded him. "And I think we might both feel safer on the other side of the border."

He settled back against the pillow, looking almost boyish with his chestnut hair falling onto his forehead. Randy had rarely seen him with a hair out of place, and it surprised her that she found his dishevelment attractive. She suppressed a smile at the thought of her meticulous Hugh trying to fight his way out of an Amazon jungle.

"Why would we be safer?" he asked. "Because of Santeras? Don't concern yourself about him, Randy. The man's all show. It's nothing but bravado."

"Hugh, he tried to torture information out of me! And he accused you of trying to bribe him."

"That grandiose bastard." An angry flush stained Hugh's face. "Carlos Santeras is a world-class crook, and he has the gall to suggest that I was trying to rig the bids on the hotel deal. I was simply speaking the man's language, dealing with him at a level I thought he'd understand. He makes a good show of moral outrage, but I hope you weren't taken in by him. There's no one more righteous than a converted sinner."

"What are you saying, Hugh? That you did offer him some kind of bribe?"

"I wouldn't have put it in those terms exactly." He seemed surprised at her concern, as well as defensive. "I was playing the game according to what I thought the rules were, *his* rules. When in Rome, that sort of thing." He broke off, shrugging. "Surely you understand, Miranda?"

"Well, yes, I—" She was trying to agree with him, trying to smile, but she couldn't. When in Rome? There was something too convenient about that logic, but she couldn't bring herself to debate it with him while he was lying in a hospital bed. Anyway, who was she to be questioning Hugh's ethics, considering what she'd done the night before?

Still, it bothered her that Hugh had thought it necessary to play Santeras's game at all. They'd always been in sync when it came to their goals. He'd once told her how attractive he found her "romantic ambition" and her "passion to succeed." She didn't know who had changed, her or Hugh. But bribing someone, even a crook, didn't seem romantic to her at all.

"Shouldn't we be getting ready to go?" Hugh asked. "We've got a plane to catch." He tried a devilish wink, but it came off looking comic with his glasses, like a Groucho Marx gag. "Not to mention our date with the man in black."

"Black?" Randy's mind flashed an image of a hooded executioner.

"The minister, silly girl. Our wedding."

"Oh . . . yes." Randy glanced out the window at the pouring rain. "Our wedding."

"Why did I choose such an elaborate wedding gown?" Randy lifted her sheer lace veil out of the way as she struggled to rearrange the voluminous skirt of her gown. She and Barb, who was to be her only attendant, had been stranded in the anteroom of the church for several minutes, trying to get her dress to behave properly.

Barb knelt and tugged the taffeta material free of the stiff undernetting it was caught on. "There," she said, smoothing the material with a reassuring smile. "You're beautiful. Now, are you about ready? Your groom awaits."

Randy took a sustaining breath. "I'm ready," she said. With a quick nod, she signaled Barb to go ahead of her, and then she herself stepped up to the chapel entrance. A moment later, as the first crashing strains of Lohengrin's wedding march sounded, she started slowly down the flower-festooned center aisle of St. Andrew's Presbyterian church.

Her ankle-length skirt swished loudly as she walked, but it was her heartbeat that sounded truly thunderous. One false step and she would be inextricably entangled in taffeta, brought down by her own bridal gown. The prospect of embarrassing herself that way in front of Hugh's family was unthinkable, especially when she was already making herself conspicuous by walking down the aisle alone.

The Pasadena Hargroves had belonged to St. Andrew's for generations. Of Hugh's immediate family, only his mother was alive. Katherine Hargrove had been infirm for years and was unable to attend the ceremony, but his aunts, uncles, cousins, and more distant relations had turned out in great numbers. And they were all scrutinizing her now, she supposed, trying to figure out what their brilliant and successful Hugh saw in her.

As she continued down the aisle, Randy tried to focus on Hugh's admiring smile instead of the sea of curious faces. She hoped he wouldn't wink again. She didn't care much for the way Hugh winked, though she couldn't imagine why she was worrying about that now.

It seemed an eternity, but once she reached the altar, Hugh took her hand and drew her alongside him. Randy's palm was damp against his, and her heart was not only pounding by that time, it seemed to be trying to escape her chest altogether. Wedding day jitters, she told herself.

Since their return from South America she'd been caught up in a frantic whirl of activity to bring the wedding off as planned. She hadn't had a moment to think of anything else, which was exactly the way she wanted it. But the pace had taken its toll. She hadn't been eating or sleeping well. She'd felt hollow all morning, nearly sick with nerves.

She clutched Hugh's hand tighter as the minister began to speak, his sonorous tones carrying all the way to the collection baskets in the back of the church. "We are gathered here together to unite this young couple in holy wedlock," he informed the crowd.

For an instant Randy's breath seemed suspended in her throat. She had waited her whole life to hear those words, to experience this moment. It was the most important day of her life, she told herself, and she wanted to enjoy every second of it, to remember it forever. She drew in a calming breath, ordering herself to relax, but the admonition didn't work. She couldn't seem to inhale normally. The air was crowding up high in her throat as if some blockage kept it from reaching her lungs.

She hung on to Hugh's hand determinedly, trying to absorb his calm presence. As the minister continued his recitation she forced herself to focus on what he was saying. His voice was melodious and soothing, but for some reason he seemed to be repeating the same words over and over again . . . *unite this couple in holy wedlock*. The phrase resounded in Randy's mind like a gunshot in a canyon.

A rush of blood through her head made her dizzy, and she knew something must be terribly wrong. She wanted to blame it on exhaustion. But the viselike blockage in her throat told her it was something far worse, something unthinkable. This was the wedding of her dreams, the culmination of all her fantasies, and yet she had a terrible urge to bolt and run from the church. She didn't want to be here!

Nerves, she told herself. Wedding day jitters. She'd waited her entire life for this day! She couldn't possibly want to ruin it.

She glanced at Hugh, desperately needing reassurance. He squeezed her hand and smiled. Her answering smile froze on her lips as she saw him wink at her—not once but several times! And then her eyes began to play terrible tricks on her. For one bewildering second she imagined that Hugh's head was encased in an executioner's hood and that he was winking at her through the eyehole!

She felt a sharp tug against her wrist and blinked to clear her vision.

"Miranda, are you all right?" Hugh was whispering. "Why are you staring at me like that? What is it?"

She blinked again, several times, and the room flashed back into focus, clearing up as quickly as it went out of kilter. Hugh was peering at her through his tortoiseshell glasses, the minister was intoning solemnly, and everything seemed as if it were back to normal.

Everything but her. She was trembling, shaking hard.

"If anyone objects to this union," the minister boomed, "let him speak now or forever hold his peace."

The chapel went still as death. . . .

Randy could hardly breathe for the silence. In her mind she heard Geoff Dias calling out an objection, storming up to the alter to carry her off. Was that what she wanted? To be rescued, kidnapped from St. Andrew's on her own wedding day?

She gripped Hugh's hand more tightly, as if by holding on to him, she could hold back the turmoil building inside her, smother it between their clasped hands. She wanted to be married to Hugh. She had *always* wanted to be married to Hugh.

"I'm fine," she whispered, aware that Hugh was still watching her with concern.

The minister nodded as if he'd heard her and continued, unfazed. Clearly he had seen worse disruptions than this one in his time, Randy realized. She shuddered with relief. If she could just hang on a little longer, it would all be over. Once they were married, she would be fine. It was the ceremony that was making her nervous, all the pomp and circumstance.

Hugh's voice startled her until she realized he was repeating a passage they'd picked out especially for this ceremony. She forced herself to smile as he said his lines and then she repeated her own lines, words she'd rehearsed by rote. Never mind that her heart felt frozen solid, that her voice sounded distant and hollow. She would be fine once this was over.

"Miranda?" the minister asked her at last. "Do you take this man to be your lawfully wedded husband, to have and to hold from this day forward, to . . ."

Randy began to nod before he'd even finished. Yes, she did, she did. But before she had a chance to say it aloud, the chapel doors swung open and the sound exploded like a bomb in her head.

She whirled, her heart surging. *"Geoff!"*

In confusion, she watched a mother and her small child slip into a pew at the back and smile sheepishly.

Late arrivals, Randy realized, stunned. She'd been

expecting to see a beautiful, angry man in fatigues, his golden hair ablaze as he strode up the aisle toward her. Now the entire church was gaping at her; even the religious figures suspended in the stained glass windows seemed to be gasping in surprise.

"Miranda?"

Hugh's horrified voice dragged at her, and the guests' eyes, round with startlement, swam in her head. What had just happened? Had she shrieked his name aloud? *Had she cried out Geoff Dias's name?*

Hugh reached for her, but she fended off his hands. Her mind was spinning, pinwheeling in a desperate need to seize on something that made sense, something that explained what was happening.

"Miranda, for God's sake!"

"I'm sorry," she blurted, the words searing her throat. "Something's wrong, terribly wrong." She turned to Hugh, and tears set fire to her eyelids, blurring his angry, reddening features. "Forgive me, Hugh, *please* forgive me. I'm not feeling well."

"What is it?" he demanded. "Miranda, what's wrong with you?"

She began to weep softly, anguish rising inside her. What *was* wrong with her? She had no good reason, no rational explanation for what she was doing. It felt as if she were giving up everything she'd worked for, throwing it all away. But she couldn't do anything else. She couldn't go through with it. "I can't do this," she told him. "I'm sorry."

"Can't do what?"

"Marry . . . you."

"Have you gone crazy?" he hissed.

"Yes, I think so," she said, her voice catching on a sob. "I really think I have gone crazy."

He tried to grab her as she stumbled backward, but she twisted away from him and hurried blindly down the steps and up the aisle toward the chapel doors. She felt as if the walls were closing in on her, as if the roof were coming down on her head, and she had a terrible, desperate need to be outside in the daylight, to be free.

Sunlight blinded her as she burst out of the church.

Fearful that Hugh and the others might follow her, she slipped into a narrow alleyway that she hoped would take her to the parking lot at the back of the church. And then she remembered that she'd come with Barb. She had no car!

Frantic, she turned into an adjoining alley, having no idea where it would lead her or what she intended to do. Her ankles wobbled as she tried to hold up her skirts and negotiate rocks and the crumbling asphalt in high heels, but she had to get away, as far away as possible. A cluster of little girls playing with dolls looked up at her as she lurched past them in her wedding gown. "She's beautiful," one of them whispered. "Just like my Barbie."

Randy began to cry all over again.

The alley opened onto a side street. Stopping to catch her breath, she lifted her veil and flung it back over her headpiece. She wiped at her eyes, undoubtedly smearing her makeup into a hopeless mess. But before she could get the flow of tears stemmed, she heard a frighteningly familiar sound—the rolling thunder of a big motorcycle.

"On, no," she moaned, refusing to look up for a moment.

The thunder came to a stop across the street from her, and when she finally brought her head up, she saw exactly what she'd been dreading. Geoff Dias was standing there, leaning against his parked Harley and gazing at her intently, his arms casually folded. "I guess I missed the wedding," he observed.

"That makes two of us." Randy gathered up her skirts and turned around, heading back down the alley. She was in no shape to deal with him now! How had he found her, anyway? He must have been following her, lying in wait. After the way they'd parted company in

Rio, it wouldn't have surprised her if he'd come to gloat over her misfortune.

She heard the roar of the Harley's engine behind her as she walked down the alley. The point was he *had* found her, and he wasn't the type who was discouraged easily.

He rolled up alongside her on the bike, dogging her unsteady footsteps. "Why the tears?" he asked, throttling the engine down.

"Because I just walked out of my own wedding, that's why! There! Are you happy? I didn't marry Mr. Fortune Five Hundred."

"As a matter of fact, I am happy. Why don't you get on the bike, Randy. We need to talk."

"No!"

"I'm not going anywhere until we do."

As they continued down the alley, she in a tearstained wedding gown, he on a massive motorcycle, she was aware of how similar this situation was to the first time they met. She was reasonably sure he'd noticed it too.

"Are you going to stop and talk?" he pressed.

Randy hushed him, realizing they were nearing the circle of little girls, all of whom were watching them, wide-eyed with interest.

"Are you going to marry *him*, lady?" one of them asked, gazing up at Geoff with wonder in her eyes. Randy knew just how the child felt, but she wasn't about to admit it.

"No," Randy assured her, "I most certainly am not."

A redheaded moppet with a squeaky voice jumped up and offered her doll, outfitted in a wedding dress. "If she doesn't want to marry you, mister, my Dream Bride Barbie will!"

"Well, thank you, sweetheart," Geoff said. "That's real tempting, but"—he indicated Randy with an offhand grin—"this one's got my heart."

"Too bad for you," the redhead commiserated. "She looks kinda mean."

Geoff exhaled a gust of laughter. "Treat me right," he told Randy under his breath. "You have a competitor for my affections."

Randy stared at him in shock, missing the humor altogether. What was that thing he'd said about having his heart?

He revved the bike's engine until it roared, then spun around in front of her. "Get on the bike, Randy," he said softly.

"No, thank you."

"Get on the bike."

Randy glanced at the little girls, aware of their rapt anticipation. Their hushed excitement echoed her own, she realized. Why was her heart pounding? And why did this feel like one of the single most frightening moments of her life? She could have been drinking champagne at a fabulous reception by now!

With the craziest feeling that she didn't want to disappoint the redheaded moppet with the bride doll, Randy gathered up her skirts and got on the bike behind Geoff. The girls gasped in concert, and she could hear their squeals above the roar of the engine as the Harley sped off.

"Where are we going?" she called out, taffeta bunched up to her chin as she clung to Geoff's denim jacket.

"I've got something to show you," he said.

They swooped down a freeway exit, flew through the tree-lined streets of exclusive San Marino and on into the foothills of the San Gabriel mountains before Geoff slowed the motorcycle. Randy was more than curious as he pulled onto the grounds of an estate that had gone badly to seed. The grass was a foot high, the rose gardens overgrown, and the main house, a once-stately English Tudor with turrets and shuttered windows, was in a state of terrible disrepair.

Geoff parked the bike in the driveway of a small stone house just behind the mansion. "The caretaker's cottage," he told Randy, helping her off the passenger seat.

"Who lives here?" she asked, following him to the door.

"Nobody has in a couple of years." He took a key from under a clay pot on the steps, unlocked the front door, and waved her inside. "I was the last tenant."

"You?" She stepped into the cottage, squinting to see in the darkness. She could make out some furniture with dust covers, but little else.

As Geoff moved around the room, opening the shuttered windows and letting the sunlight pour in, Randy saw an image that astonished her. On the wall opposite her was a picture of someone familiar. Thinking her eyes were playing tricks on her again, she blinked to clear her vision. That's when she realized the entire wall was a gallery of women in various poses, some of them erotic, all of them beautiful . . . all of them her.

"What is this?" she asked, barely able to speak. The words floated out of her, as light and dizzy as she was.

"Somebody I met once." He stood back, as if wanting to give her some space. "A gypsy bride."

"You did this, all of them?"

He nodded. "I'm the tormented artist. I had nothing else to remember you by," he said, his voice going husky. "Nothing but the images in my head. At first I thought I could release them that way, exorcise them by getting them on paper, but it didn't work. Nothing worked."

Something strange was happening to Randy's heart. It had been going too fast before, but now it was slowing, hardening, hurting, as if in anticipation of some future disaster. She knew what was happening to her. She just couldn't believe it. She was falling—no, *plummeting*—for a mercenary soldier with holes in his pants. For a biker! Oh, Edna!

Randy's heartstrings pulled even tighter as she caught a flash of sweet, sexy need in Geoff's eyes. Why was he looking at her that way? As if he wanted to take her in his arms and hold her tight. As if his heart was hurting too.

She turned back to the gallery, searching for something that would release her from the turmoil that was building inside her. But just as the artwork hadn't released him, it couldn't free her either. They were images of a woman who was frightened and rebellious, a woman who was fiery and sad and love-be-damned angry. He had caught every angle, revealing things about her she barely knew herself . . . the heartbroken bride, the yearning child who'd always wanted a shiny swing set. He had touched the soul of Randy Witherspoon—sad child, proud woman, survivor.

"I love you, Randy," he said softly. "I do, baby."

"Oh, Geoff—" She turned to him, tears welling, silently pleading with him *not* to love her, *not to make her love him.*

The anguish she felt was filling her heart with choked pain. "What will become of me?" she asked. "I don't want to live like Edna—all those men leaving her, longing for something she never got—and I don't want to die like her either."

"You're not Edna, Randy. And I'm not all those men."

Randy could hear herself breathing, raspy, aching. She could hear him breathing, too, and hardly knew which was which—his breath or hers?

"Let go of the past, Randy," he urged. "It's Edna's past you're clinging to, it's Edna's dream. Let go of all that and deal with what's happening here, now. Deal with us."

She shook her head, laughing sadly, torn. A biker? One of Edna's men? This was too crazy to be believed. She could hear his voice echoing in her head, the incredible things he said to her that night in the alley in Rio. *The "baby" on my bike is singular. It's you, Randy. Baby, it's you.*

"What do you want, gypsy?" he asked. "Who do you want?"

A terrible, aching lump closed her throat as she looked up at him and nodded. "You." It was a commitment that both freed her and paralyzed her with fear, an acknowledgment that she was going to risk it all. She shuddered as he started toward her.

"You aren't going to break my heart, are you, Geoff?" she asked brokenly, smiling through the tears that washed her face. "You aren't going to love me and leave me?"

He pulled her into his arms and held her tightly, his heart hammering against hers. "No, baby, no," he said, pressing his lips to her hair, cradling her against him with a tenderness that must have sprung from the pain of his own needs. "I'm not going to do any of those things," he promised. "I've been loving you too long for that."

He held her for a long time, just held her, both of them seeming to need that kind of comfort. Finally he turned her face up and brushed her lips with the warmth of his.

She moaned with the sweetness of it. And then the tender touches of his mouth deepened to a kiss that burned with passion and promise. It held the startlement of sudden love and the harsh, sweet truth of dreams . . . their dreams?

When Randy opened her eyes and looked up at him, she saw so many things that she had never allowed herself to acknowledge before. He was a good man, even a gentle man. He had the sensitivity of an artist and the honesty and integrity to live a life based on his own beliefs and convictions. Biker or not, he was a better man than Hugh, she realized, surprised that she'd been so blinded by her need to see people as she believed them to be, rather than who they actually were.

"I love you," she said, barely able to get the words out.

He laughed. "Don't make it sound so painful."

"It is . . . I'm so frightened."

"Then that makes two of us."

Another myth exploded, she realized, gazing into his eyes. Geoff Dias could be frightened. He was as fearful of opening his heart to her as she was to him, as eager to be accepted and loved for who he was. *Edna, I've found him,* she thought, tears burning her eyelids. *I've found the prince.*

Her welling tears spilled over, flooding his fingers as he tried to dry them. "I love you," she told him again, and this time the words ached with heartfelt conviction.

Moments later, with a shaky sigh, she turned in his arms, needing to look at the pictures again, to drink in their moody brush strokes and dreamy eroticism. "I haunted you so much that you had to paint me?" she asked him, still not quite able to believe it. "Over and over again? That's terribly romantic."

"That's me," he laughed, "a terribly romantic guy."

They were silent for a while, holding each other, reminded of their past by its evidence on the wall . . . until he released her and walked to one of the cottage windows. "Come here," he said, holding out his hand. "I've got something else to show you."

Randy knew what he was going to say even before she joined him. "This is yours, isn't it?" she asked him, looking out at the neglected grounds and the Tudor mansion.

"It's mine now. My parents left it to me."

Sensing his reluctance to talk about what had happened, she turned her attention back to the window. "If you'd rather not, Geoff—"

"No, I want to . . . but prepare yourself. It gets pretty ugly." He drew her close, pulling her into the crook of his arm as he stared out the window. "My father committed suicide when I was sixteen. He was a partner in a Wall Street brokerage, and he got embroiled in a financial scandal before those things were fashionable. He was too proud to go to prison, too proud to do anything but put a gun to his head, apparently."

"Oh, Geoff, I'm sorry."

He nodded as if to say it was all right. "My mother never recovered," he told her after a space of silence. "Two months later, she was dead too. An overdose of sleeping pills. The doctors said it was accidental, but I knew she didn't want to live without him. They were that close. Sometimes even I felt like an intruder."

Randy laid her hand over his and looked up at him. "What did you do?"

"I lived with an uncle for a while, finished high school, even gave college a shot. My father's family was originally from northern Spain. They came here dirt-poor, with nothing to their names but their belief in the American dream. They made their fortune here, so naturally, I was expected to restore the family's honor, carry on the proud tradition. They'd assumed I'd become a broker, or if not that, a lawyer. Maybe even a hotel magnate, like Hugh."

She was beginning to understand his antipathy toward the things she'd wanted desperately, and especially toward her former fiancé.

"Not everyone gets an up-close and personal look at the dark side of material success," he explained. "I saw how wealth bred the desire for more to the point that even a man like my father could become corrupted. It wasn't his sense of honor that killed him, it was shame. In his suicide note he admitted he was guilty of everything he'd been accused of."

Geoff exhaled heavily. "So I said to hell with it all and joined the Marines."

She turned in his arms to face him, wishing she knew how to convey the compassion she felt. "I'm sorry, Geoff. That must have been terrible for you, to lose your parents, to lose everything."

"It was rough," he admitted. "I was a big, strapping kid, but I *was* a kid, and it hurt like hell."

He kissed her lightly as if to assure her that time had healed the wounds, that he was okay now. "There's just

one thing you need to understand. I didn't lose everything. There's still a lot of money involved. It's being
managed by attorneys, held in trust . . . for me."

"For you? A lot of money? You're—"

"Rich, I think you could say." He grimaced. "Filthy."

"Why didn't you tell me?"

"What would you have done if I had? I didn't want to
have to compete with that dream of yours. Or to be put
in the position of having to outbid Hugh for your
affections."

The man had a point, she admitted. Being Hugh's
wife had become an obsession. He'd been her fantasy of
the perfect man, the answer to all her fears and inse-
curities. She had come terrifyingly close to marrying
him as it was. Her only regret was that it had taken her
so long to see the mistake she was making, and that
she'd had to hurt Hugh before it was over. She regretted
that deeply.

"Still love me?" Geoff asked, tilting her chin up and
dazzling her with his emerald green eyes. "Just checking." His mouth curved into the slow, sexy smile that
never failed to make her heartbeat go weak.

"Oh, I suppose," she said, sighing as if it were a
terrible burden. "I've got to be honest, though. I'm not
sad you have lots of disgusting money, but I think I
could have been blissfully happy with the poverty-
stricken artist. As long as he drew pictures only of me."

"Umm," he said, nipping her lower lip. "I've already
got an idea for the first pose."

Randy pretended to be frightened. "Is there leather
involved?"

Epilogue

One month later . . .

Randy tilted her face to the sky and breathed deeply, bathing her senses with fresh, sweet mountain air. Sunlight flickered brightly through the branches of a huge old sycamore as she walked around to the back of Chase and Annie Beaudine's mountain home, a charmingly rustic cabin nestled in the foothills of Wyoming's Wind River range. Her mission was to find the three men who were AWOL from the small anniversary party going on inside the cabin.

A roan mare nickered at her from its paddock as Randy passed by. She took it as a friendly overture, but didn't stop to chat. Being a city girl, she'd had very little experience with animals who were bigger than she was, and now didn't seem the time to test the horse's good humor.

She spotted the missing persons in a grassy meadow that lay beyond the barn. Shirtless and shoeless in the dazzling sunshine, the three men were playing football as only ex-Marine buddies could. She stopped to watch as Chase Beaudine speed-hiked the football to Johnny Starhawk, then sprinted out to catch Johnny's pass. Chase darted, dodged, and feinted, amazingly agile for a big man as he tried to outmaneuver Geoff, who was guarding him doggedly.

The football soared toward the clouds, a Hail Mary pass if ever Randy had seen one. Chase faked to the right, evading Geoff long enough to leap into the air as the ball dropped out of the sky. Just as Chase's questing fingers were about to seize the prize, a bare foot flashed out of nowhere and karate-kicked the ball into oblivion. Geoff had launched himself like a weapon, using a spinning side kick to intercept Johnny's pass.

Randy had to restrain herself from cheering.

Chase and Johnny howled in protest. "You can't do that!" Chase complained.

"Does this look like a boxing ring, Dias?" Johnny shouted.

Geoff's reckless grin became a grimace as his opponents rushed him, knocked him to the ground, and piled on top of him. A wrestling match resulted, and when the horseplay threatened to get out of hand, Randy decided it was time to break things up.

"*Gentle*men!" she called out, putting a drill instructor's spin on the word. "There's a party going on up at the house, in case you've forgotten. It's time to open the gifts."

A short time later she had the deserters in tow. They'd washed up at the faucet alongside the barn at her suggestion, and as she herded them into the cabin, she felt like a stern schoolteacher escorting the class troublemakers to the principal's office.

"Here's Daddy!" Annie Beaudine cried, plunking a red-headed baby into Chase's arms the moment he entered the cabin. Their other child, a strawberry blond toddler, squealed in delight, attaching herself to Chase's leg. Chase seemed a little embarrassed by all the attention, but it was clear he was also delighted by it.

Randy's throat tightened at the tender way he scooped the toddler up and nuzzled her hair, kissing the child's blond curls. His show of affection had a bittersweet effect on Randy. It stirred up old longings for the father she never had, but it also instilled in her the hope and the silent resolution that her own children would be as fortunate. Chase's girls were very lucky to have a father who so obviously adored them.

Geoff hooked an arm around Randy and drew her close. "I want a half-dozen of those," he murmured softly in her ear. Desire shimmered warmly in his eyes as he looked down at her. "What do you say?"

"A half-dozen kids?" Randy nestled into the crook of his arm and laughed weakly. "Don't you think maybe we should get married first?"

"Listen up, folks." Annie Beaudine clinked her glass of iced tea with a fork, calling the small crowd to attention. "Honor and Johnny, our happily married couple of one whole year, want to open their gifts. Right, you two?"

Honor was sitting next to Johnny Starhawk on the couch, and Randy thought she had never seen a more striking couple. Honor was as fair and lovely as Johnny was dark and arrestingly handsome. They looked as if they had been brought together by the same elemental forces that made magnetic poles attract, as if they were bound by their extraordinary differences. Their children would be something to see, Randy realized, drawn to the couple although she'd met them only that day.

Honor abandoned all pretense of ladylike restraint as she opened the presents, oohing and aahing over items that made ingenious use of the tradition of paper for first-anniversary gifts. Chase and Annie gave them a set of self-help books for young married couples, including an *Intimate Dinners for Two* cookbook and a primer on sensual massage. While Honor continued to unwrap packages, Johnny leafed through the books, promising her a very special evening when they got home.

Randy had no doubt that he could provide such an evening. He was possessed of the most riveting natural sensuality she'd ever seen in a man. He was also clearly madly in love with his beautiful, gentle wife.

Geoff waited until they'd finished with the other gifts before presenting Johnny with a special offering—an oil

painting he'd made of Chase, Johnny, and himself in
their early mercenary days. Randy recognized the
painting as a replica of a snapshot Geoff carried in his
wallet. The three ex-Marines were sitting in a bar
somewhere, probably an exotic foreign port, celebrating
their first recovery mission. The media had not yet
discovered the trio they would later dub the "Stealth
Commandos," but Randy could see the potential for
heroism in each one of them. In his military fatigues,
cropped hair, and aviator sunglasses, Geoff looked
young and reckless, flushed with the thrill of victory.

Johnny seemed to be struggling with emotion as he
studied the picture, and even Chase looked slightly
shaken by it. Finally Johnny composed himself enough
to glance up and grin at Geoff. "You got my hair wrong,
you chump. I never wore it that short."

Laughter broke the tension as Johnny sprang up and
gave Geoff a bear hug, thanking him for the painting.
Randy's heart was in her throat before the two men
released each other. And then Chase joined them,
clapping Geoff on the back affectionately and kidding
Johnny about needing a haircut. Randy could feel the
genuine warmth between all three men, and she hoped
they would always be as close as they were this day.

As Geoff returned to her side she felt a rush of love
that impelled her to clasp his hand tightly and squeeze
it. How had she ever had the good fortune to find—or be
found by—a man with so many wonderful dichotomies
in his nature? He was tough and tender, strong and
gentle, all of the traits a woman sought and cherished
in a man, and yet on a deeper level, he had an affinity
for human nature that allowed him to mirror a person's
soul in his work. There was a depth of understanding in
him that made him all the more mysterious to her, all
the more attractive.

As the party continued, Honor convinced her father-
in-law Chy Starhawk, an Apache medicine man, to
share his gift for prophecy with the crowd. With his long

hair hovering like a white cloud around his shoulders, the shaman turned first to Geoff and Randy. A mysterious smile deepened the grooves of his sepia-colored skin.

"There is brightness around you both," he said, studying them for a moment. "Like the light of day glowing through an overcast sky. It's the brightness of a promise, of believing in things you can't see with your eyes." He hesitated, as if caught in the awareness, but not fully understanding it. "I see the sparkle of sunlight on deep green water."

"Maybe the brightness has something to do with this." Geoff took a small box from his shirt pocket and offered it to Randy, an expectant smile on his face.

Randy drew in a sharp breath as she opened the box. Nestled in lush white velvet was the most exquisite emerald ring she'd ever seen. Her hand flew to her mouth, trying to contain the surprise that trembled there.

"It was my grandmother's," Geoff explained, lowering his voice to an intimate level as he drew her into his arms. "My father gave it to my mother when they were engaged. I wanted you to have it. I'm sure they would have too."

Randy could feel the ring's brightness in her heart. It was as piercingly sharp as her feelings for him, and she wanted to believe that its rich light was a symbol of the love that would sustain them through everything, even the darker times that were in store for every relationship. In truth, she was still frightened of loving Geoff Dias, but she knew he harbored fears too. The loss of his parents had made him wary of a deep and committed bond, and yet he was willing to risk taking that step now, willing to risk everything. If he could open his heart to the dangers of loving a woman, then surely she could surrender hers to the fearful sweetness of trusting a man.

The light would sustain them.

The light was love.

THE EDITOR'S CORNER

Next month LOVESWEPT presents an Easter parade of six fabulous romances. Not even April showers can douse the terrific mood you'll be in after reading each and every one of these treasures.

The hero of Susan Connell's new LOVESWEPT, #606, is truly **SOME KIND OF WONDERFUL.** As mysterious and exciting as the Greek islands he calls home, Alex Stoner is like a gorgeous god whose mouth promises pagan pleasures. He's also a cool businessman who never lets a woman get close. But prim and proper Sandy Patterson, widow of his college roommate, is unlike any he's ever known, and he sets out to make her ache for his own brand of passion. Susan takes you on a roller coaster of emotion with this romance.

Kay Hooper continues her MEN OF MYSTERIES PAST series with **HUNTING THE WOLFE,** LOVESWEPT #607. Security expert Wolfe Nickerson appeared in the first book in the series, **THE TOUCH OF MAX,** LOVESWEPT #595, and in this new novel, he almost finds himself bested by a pint-sized computer programmer. Storm Tremaine blows into his life like a force of nature, promising him the chase of his life . . . and hinting she's fast enough to catch him! When he surrenders to her womanly charms, he doesn't know that Storm holds a secret . . . a secret that could forever destroy his trust. Kay is at her best with this terrific love story.

BREATHLESS, LOVESWEPT #608 by Diane Pershing, is how Hollis Blake feels when Tony Stellini walks into her gift shop. The tall, dark, and sensuous lawyer makes the air sizzle with his wildfire energy, and for the first time Hollis longs to taste every pleasure she's never had, pursue all the dreams she's been denied. Her innocence stirs an overpowering desire in Tony, but he senses that with this untouched beauty, he has to take it one slow, delicious step at a time. This is a romance to relish, a treat from Diane.

Linda Cajio begins **DANCING IN THE DARK,** LOVE-SWEPT #609, with an eye-opening scene in which the hero is engaged in a sacred ceremony and dancing naked in the woods! Jake Halford feels a little silly performing the men's movement ritual, but Charity Brown feels downright embarrassed at catching him at it. How can she ever work with her company's new vice president without remembering the thrilling sight of his muscles and power? The way Linda has these two learning how to mix business and pleasure is a pure delight.

HANNAH'S HUNK, LOVESWEPT #610 by Sandra Chastain, is nothing less than a sexy rebel with a southern drawl . . . and an ex-con whom Hannah Clendening "kidnaps" so he could pose for the cover of her Fantasy Romance. Dan Bailey agrees, but only if Hannah plays the heroine and he gets to kiss her. When desire flares between them like a force field, neither believes that what they feel could last. Of course Sandra, with her usual wit and charm, makes sure there's a happily ever after for this unusual couple.

Finally, there's **THE TROUBLE WITH MAGIC,** LOVE-SWEPT #611 by Mary Kay McComas. Harriet Wheaton has an outrageous plan to keep Payton Dunsmore from foreclosing on the great manor house on Jovette Island. Marooning them there, she tells him that she's trying to fulfill the old legend of enemies meeting on Jovette and falling in love! Payton's furious at first, but he soon succumbs to the enchantment of the island . . . and Harriet herself. Mary Kay delivers pure magic with this marvelous romance.

On sale this month from FANFARE are four outstanding novels. If you missed **TEMPERATURES RISING** by blockbuster author Sandra Brown when it first came out, now's your chance to grab a copy of this wonderfully evocative love story. Chantal duPont tells herself that she needs Scout Ritland only to build a much-needed bridge on the South Pacific island she calls home. And when the time comes for him to leave, she must make the painful decision of letting him go—or risking everything by taking a chance on love.

From beloved author Rosanne Bittner comes **OUTLAW HEARTS,** a stirring new novel of heart-stopping danger and burning desire. At twenty, Miranda Hayes has known more than her share of heartache and loss. Then she clashes with the notorious gunslinger Jake Harkner, a hard-hearted loner with a price on his head, and finds within herself a deep well of courage . . . and feelings of desire she's never known before.

Fanfare is proud to publish **THE LAST HIGHWAYMAN,** the first historical romance by Katherine O'Neal, a truly exciting new voice in women's fiction. In this delectable action-packed novel, Christina has money, power, and position, but she has never known reckless passion, never found enduring love . . . until she is kidnapped by a dangerously handsome bandit who needs her to heal his tormented soul.

In the bestselling tradition of Danielle Steel, **CONFI-DENCES** by Penny Hayden is a warm, deeply moving novel about four "thirty-something" mothers whose lives are interwoven by a long-held secret—a secret that could now save the life of a seventeen-year-old boy dying of leukemia.

Also available now in the hardcover edition from Double-day is **MASK OF NIGHT** by Lois Wolfe, a stunning historical novel of romantic suspense. When an actress and a cattle rancher join forces against a diabolical villain, the result is an unforgettable story of love and vengeance.

Happy reading!

With warmest wishes,

Nita Taublib

Nita Taublib
Associate Publisher
LOVESWEPT and FANFARE

Don't miss these fabulous
Bantam
Women's Fiction
titles
on sale in FEBRUARY

TEMPERATURES RISING
by Sandra Brown

OUTLAW HEARTS
by Rosanne Bittner

THE LAST HIGHWAYMAN
by Katherine O'Neal

CONFIDENCES
by Penny Hayden

In hardcover from Doubleday,
MASK OF NIGHT
by Lois Wolfe
author of THE SCHEMERS

From the *New York Times*
bestselling author of
A Whole New Light and *The Texas! Trilogy*

Sandra Brown
TEMPERATURES RISING

In this wonderfully evocative love story, a man and a woman from vastly different worlds are brought together on a lush South Pacific island.

Chantal duPont loved her tropical island home and would do anything she could to protect it from the greed of outsiders. To her the developers of the new Coral Reef resort were the enemy, plain and simple. So when she devised a plan to save her village, she never expected to come up against a man like Scout Ritland. She told herself that she only needed Scout to build a much-needed bridge for her people. But as the days pass and the work progresses, Chantal has to face the possibility that Scout means more to her than she had thought. And when the time comes for him to leave, she will have to make the painful decision to let him go—or risk everything by taking a chance on love.

OUTLAW HEARTS
by
Rosanne Bittner

**From the author of THUNDER ON THE PLAINS comes
the sweeping, heart-stirring saga of a man who lived by the
gun and the daring young woman who taught him how to
love. . . .**

*At twenty, Miranda Hayes had known more than her share of heartache
and loss. Widowed by the war, orphaned by a vicious band of rebel
raiders, she was a woman alone in a harsh, unyielding frontier. Then she
clashed with the notorious gunslinger Jake Harkner, a hard-hearted loner
with a price on his head, and found within herself a deep well of
courage . . . and feelings of desire she'd never known.*

*Hunted by lawmen and desperadoes alike, haunted by his brutal past,
Jake had spent a lifetime on the dusty trail—and on the run. Until he met
a vibrant, honey-haired beauty who was determined to change his violent
ways, who loved him enough to risk her life to be his woman . . . an
outlaw's woman.*

*From the vast plains of the Midwest across the Oregon Trail to the
sun-drenched valleys of southern California, from the blazing Nevada
desert to the boomtowns of Colorado, Miranda and Jake struggled to
endure amid the perils of a lawless wilderness. In a world of heart-
stopping danger and burning desire, could their hard-won love survive the
shadows that stalked their happiness?*

Jake put his head back again, closing his eyes and listening to
the storm, remembering another storm, one that hit on a night
he would never forget. Should he tell her? He knew she was
wondering, and what better way to make her hate him than to
tell her the truth? The storm only brought it all back more

vividly anyway. Thunder clapped again, and he could hear the gun going off at the same time. He could see the look of astonishment on his father's face.

He waited a moment longer, another crash of thunder making him wince and put a hand to his forehead.

"Jake? What's wrong?"

He ran his hand through his hair. "Where's the whiskey I bought back at that fort?" He saw her hesitate, knew what she was thinking. Giving whiskey to an ailing man was one thing, but it was something completely different when given to a perfectly healthy man with a notorious reputation. "Don't worry. I don't react to whiskey like my pa used to," he told her, "although he didn't need alcohol to bring out the worst in him."

Miranda watched him a moment longer, then nodded toward the pile of blankets. "You're leaning against it—in the crate under those blankets."

Jake turned to search, grinning to himself at the realization she must have put it out of sight in hopes he would forget he had it. He removed a flask from the crate and uncorked it, turning back around and taking a swallow. He let it burn its way down his throat and into his stomach. He seldom drank much, hated the memories of what whiskey did to his father, how mean it made him. Still, right now it gave him the added courage he needed to shock Miranda Hayes out of any feelings she might have for him. He did not need or want to talk about this, but if it would take the light out of Miranda Hayes's eyes when she looked at him, it would be worth the telling.

He lowered the bottle, staring at it for a moment, taking another drag on the cheroot. "I killed him," he told her.

Miranda frowned, taking her gaze from her sewing and meeting his eyes. "Killed whom?"

Jake held her eyes, giving her his darkest, meanest look. "My *pa!* I shot him dead. What do you think of that?" To his frustration and amazement, he saw no shock, no animosity, no horror. He saw only a strange sorrow.

"I know," she answered. "I'm sorry, Jake."

He just stared at her a moment, astounded at her reply, suddenly angry with her. "What the hell do you mean, you *know*! And you're *sorry*? I didn't tell you in order to get your damn *pity*!" He let out a nervous laugh. "Jesus, woman, what the hell is the matter with you?"

Miranda put down the sewing. "You expected me to be surprised? After all, that always has been the rumor. After what you told me back at the cabin, I had no doubt it was true. What I'm sorry about is you must have had a good cause, which means your father must have been doing something terrible to you or to someone you loved. What did he do, Jake? Does it have something to do with Santana?"

He rolled his eyes and took another swallow of whiskey. "You're incredible, you know that? What the hell kind of a man kills his own pa?"

"A desperate one, and I'm betting he wasn't a man at all. He was probably still a boy, and sometimes that same boy comes charging out of the man, fighting, angry, defending himself, refusing to have feelings because he might hurt again, and he doesn't want to hurt. He's afraid—"

"Shut up!" He wanted her to flinch, but she didn't. Damn her! Damn slip of a woman! "Maybe what I ought to do is show you just how much of a man I *really* am!" he deliberately snarled. He turned and crammed the whiskey back into the crate, then dropped the cheroot back into the tin cup. He began unbuckling his gunbelt.

Miranda truly wondered if she had gone too far this time. The man hated it when someone saw through the outer meanness to his vulnerability. It made him furious, and a furious Jake Harkner might not be as safe as she had supposed. Had she trusted too much?

He tossed the gunbelt aside, and before Miranda could react, he lunged at her and grasped her arms tightly, painfully. Her eyes widened, and she dropped her sewing when he lifted and moved her like a ragdoll, pushing her against the blankets against which he had himself been resting. "I *want* you, Randy Hayes," he snarled. "What do you think of *that*!"

Miranda drew in her breath and faced him boldly. "I think that whatever you want to do to me, you will. After all, you're stronger than I am. Just don't take me like your father would take a woman, Jake. And don't do it just to try to scare me off, because you can't. I love you, Jake Harkner, and you damn well know it! You'd never hurt me!" Unwanted tears suddenly filled her eyes, and she felt his grip relax. He massaged her arms for a moment.

"Damn you, woman," he said softly then. "How do you know me that well?" He leaned closer, kissed her eyes, licked at her tears, found her mouth and licked at that too. Miranda found that her instinctive response to him was powerful, as though it was always supposed to be this way. She closed her eyes and met his tongue, letting him slake his own between her lips in a kiss more delicious than any kiss Mack had ever given her. Had she just been too young then to fully enjoy a man? Or perhaps she had just been too long without. She only knew this felt more wonderful than anything she had ever experienced.

Jake groaned, and his kiss grew hotter, deeper. She felt him pull a few blankets down, let him lay her down on them. Never had she wanted a man like this, with such wantonness, such an agonizing need. She returned his kisses with a fiery passion she had not known she was capable of feeling.

THE LAST HIGHWAYMAN
by
Katherine O'Neal

We are proud to publish the first historical romance by a truly exciting new voice in women's fiction!

Christina left home at sixteen to escape her parents—stars of the English theatre who exploited her brilliance as a costume designer and makeup artist, but never forgave their daughter for surviving a flu epidemic in which her twin sister died. Best friends with the wicked Oscar Wilde, and married young to an aged duke who died soon after, she has money, power, and position—but she has never known reckless passion . . . never found enduring love.

Richard is the dangerously handsome son of a Lord who married a beautiful Irish girl only to offer her to the licentious Prince of Wales in exchange for wealth and power. Sworn to avenge his mother's fate and aid the Irish rebellion against the crown, he expects only ransom when he abducts the beautiful outspoken duchess from her bedroom late one night. Instead, he finds he has captured a woman who will become known as "the bandit's bride"—a woman strong enough to heal his tormented soul, and so dazzlingly seductive in his arms she will possess his heart forever.

THE LAST HIGHWAYMAN is a delectable action-packed novel of irresistible romance and fascinating history, highly emotional and full of witty dialogue and unexpected twists.

"Going somewhere, Duchess?" the Captain asked.

She backed up against the stone wall of the forge, but he followed, keeping the sharp blade perched against her neck. He was so close that she could feel the hard contours of his body pressing into hers. Her breath was coming fast now as her mind raced. She could outsmart him, but she couldn't overpower him.

"How did you know I'd try to escape?" she gasped.

"A number of ways. You never asked why I kept you here, or for how long. I've never once known a woman who wasn't curious about her fate."

Damn! She hadn't thought of that. She lifted her chin with a show of bravado. "Well?" she demanded. "Are you going to slash my throat? Cut off my ear?"

He ran the knife along her neck in a ruminative manner. "Frankly, I can think of more interesting things to cut."

His voice was at her ear, muffled and intimate, yet hard as steel. Putting a thumb to her throat, he moved the knife and cut away the top button of her riding habit. She shivered. In the distance, she heard the men heading back for the mill. She took a breath to cry out, but he pressed himself against her in a menacing way.

"I wouldn't. They'd just assume that I was doing what I'm doing, and leave me to my spoils."

She was shaking uncontrollably. "You won't like it," she warned in a croaking voice. "I'm dead inside. I can no longer feel anything. You might as well vent your lust on a sack of meal."

He cut away the second button. "Is that why you spent last night vexing me? To show how impervious you are to desire?"

"I merely meant to distract you, to keep your mind from my escape."

He cut away the third button, opened the bodice with the point of his knife, and lowered his lips to her neck. "You did a fine job of—distracting me, I must say."

She found courage enough to taunt him. "I've over-estimated you. I wouldn't think a man like you would have to resort to rape. You disappoint me, highwayman."

He ignored her. One by one, the buttons were severed to fall on the stone floor. He undressed her slowly, as if he had all the time in the world, tossing each piece of her clothing aside.

When she was naked, he turned her so that her back was to him. He rested his left arm around the front of her shoulders so that the knife once again lay across the hollow of her throat.

Bending, he kissed her shoulder, felt her shiver against the night air. With his right hand, he stroked her belly and moved up to cup the mound of her breast. She swayed and her breath became labored.

"You're a weak-livered coward," she moaned, "forcing your attentions on women who have no interest."

His hand moved to the other breast.

"I should die of shame, knowing I had to force a woman at the point of a knife," she continued.

He brought his lips to her ear. Her breath caught in her throat as he nuzzled the side of her neck.

"I wouldn't have you if you were the last man—"

He trailed his hand along her belly and down a path to her thigh.

"Weak, despicable cad," she accused, but her voice was breathless now.

Against her will, she leaned back into him, conforming her body to his. She rubbed against him like a cat against a post.

Finally he spoke. His mouth was at her ear and his voice was deep and hushed, yet ruthlessly hard. "I've never raped a woman in my life," he informed her, his breath warming her ear. "I have no intention of starting now."

"You make a poor showing of your good intentions," she retorted in a voice crackling with passion.

"I shall give you nothing you don't ask for voluntarily. So you see, my lady, the game is up to you."

Having stated his intentions, his mouth moved once again to her shoulder. He kissed the satiny skin, making his way with infinite leisure down the quivering flesh of her arm. His hands explored her body with feathery strokes as he awaited her reply.

She sighed and dropped her head back against him. "Put your knife away, highwayman," she directed. "You'll have no need of it this night."

He was still. Then, removing the blade from her throat, he tossed the weapon into the half-roof so that it landed in a far beam with a twang.

Freed, she pivoted around and began to unbutton his shirt. "Your grace! You shock me!" he mocked.

"I'm an impatient woman, highwayman. It takes more than weapons and promises to satisfy me."

Stepping out of his boots, he asked, "Have you ever been satisfied?"

She showed her teeth in a wicked smile. "Never."

"You are about," he informed her, "to put that in the past tense."

She gave him a lusty chuckle. "Well,"—she shrugged—"I admire your confidence. You are, most certainly, welcome to try."

Any other man might have been intimidated by her challenge. He showed no sign of such quaverings. Taking her shoulders in his hands, he pulled her to him very slowly, so that her breasts just barely touched his chest, until—slowly, slowly—she could feel every rigid contour of his frame.

He kissed her with the same exquisite languor. His lips were firm, and they moved over hers with practised ease. She'd expected rape. What he was giving her was seduction. He seemed to be moving in slow motion, luxuriating in each touch, each kiss, each moan of pleasure that escaped her throat. As his hands stroked her body, igniting the long-dormant flames, he tasted of her mouth with a leisure that was devastating.

Soon, it became unbearable. Her body, denied since the ravages of the Prince, was alive with passion, with hunger, with need. She pressed herself against him, urging him on. . . .

CONFIDENCES
by
Penny Hayden

**In the bestselling tradition of Danielle Steel, CONFIDENCES
is a warm, deeply moving novel about four "thirty-something"
mothers, whose lives are interwoven by a long-held secret—a
secret that could now save the life of a seventeen-year-old boy
dying of leukemia.**

*When Douglass Sommers discovers that he needs a bone marrow trans-
plant, his parents are forced to admit that he was adopted. It is his
desperate search for his biological mother and father that triggers the
compelling stories of four very different women who are the closest of
friends, yet who have something important to discover about themselves
as mothers—and as women. Their separate trials and struggles for love
and passion are powerfully portrayed in this wise, poignant novel that
captures all the drama and complexities of modern love.*

July

SAN FRANCISCO

It wasn't anyone's fault. At least that was what Mom and Dad
and his doctor kept telling him. It wasn't his fault; it wasn't his
parents' fault; there wasn't a damn thing to blame except some
stupid cells gone crazy.

Turning his face toward the hospital room window, Doug
Sommers blinked hard to keep back the tears stinging his eyes.
He wished everyone would leave so he could cry instead of
having to act so goddamn brave all over the place. He was only
seventeen, for Christ's sake. He didn't want to die.

While Dr. Levison droned on to Mom and Dad about white

blood cells and platelets and chemotherapy and bone marrow, Doug aimed the remote control at the television and zapped it on, then flicked through the channels until he found MTV. By the time he got out of the hospital, summer would be over, school would have started, and there'd be a whole new bunch of songs on the top-ten list.

Some senior year. Instead of playing football, he'd be taking a mess of drugs that would make him feel even worse than he did now; instead of going out with Jennifer, he'd be getting stuck with needles and his blond hair would be falling out in handfuls. He'd read *Brian's Song* in seventh grade—he knew what to expect: first they tortured you; then you died. He poked a button on the control, and the television clicked off.

"So, how does that sound, Doug?" Dr. Levison's voice was low and pleasant, but direct, not at all syrupy like those doctors who went around saying, "And how are we feeling today?" He had to hand it to her; at least she was honest. She smiled at him as if she expected him to be pleased by whatever it was she'd been telling his parents.

It was easy for her. She wasn't going to die before she'd ever really lived. He shrugged, his grip tightening on the remote control as he fought the urge to heave it at the window. All he wanted to do right now was scream and cry and break things. But every time he looked at Mom and Dad, at the love and grief engraved on their faces, he tensed against the horrible rage twisting his guts, invading his blood like the malignant myeloid cells the tests had discovered. It wasn't their fault, he reminded himself again, for the hundredth time. He had to keep it together for them.

"I'm sorry," he said. "I sort of spaced out."

"I was just explaining to your parents what doctors call a *protocol*, what I think is the best treatment plan for you. The first goal is to get you into remission." Dr. Levison nodded at his parents. "That's accomplished through induction therapy—or chemotherapy, in your case. At this point we may not need to resort to radiotherapy."

"Then I won't lose my hair?" His face flushed as soon as the words were out. What the hell did it matter if he was bald when he died?

"Some drugs may make it a little thinner, but, no, you

probably won't lose it all." Her tone was serious, matter-of-fact, as if he'd asked a perfectly reasonable question. "There are a number of other possible side effects of the drugs we use to induce remission. But if we're successful, there's the possibility of a bone marrow transplant, where we replace your diseased marrow with a donor's healthy marrow. It's still experimental, but the overall results have been good, and some transplant patients are still in remission after more than eight years. I was just going to explain it to your parents. Should I come back later or are you ready to hear about it now?"

His cheeks grew even hotter. She seemed to understand how angry he was, and she didn't seem to mind at all. "I guess so," he mumbled, laying the control on the bedside table. He spread his hands out over the white covers and stared at them. Maybe it wasn't so hopeless after all. Suddenly, eight years looked like a lifetime. He could do a lot in eight years—finish high school, graduate from college, maybe even get married. At the very least, he wouldn't die a virgin; he'd make damn sure of that.

"You have a lot of points in your favor," she said. "You're young; your general physical condition is excellent; your internal organs appear to be in good shape; you've never been treated for blood cell diseases before." She turned to his parents. "The biggest consideration in bone marrow transplants, however, is finding a prospective donor, someone with a matching HL-A type. We find that out by testing the lymphocytes in the blood to see if they share the same antigens and by culturing the donor's blood with the patient's to see if the cells attack each other." She smiled at Doug. "You have two younger brothers, right?"

"Yeah." He pushed himself up straighter and cocked his head, the warmth of hope loosening the constricted, cold feeling in his chest. "But what have they got to do with it?"

"Well, an identical twin would be ideal because he would have the same chromosomal inheritance as you. But since you don't have a twin, we'll look at your brothers. Genetically speaking, there's a 25 percent chance for each one to be a good match. Parents are a possibility, too, though the chances are much slimmer."

Doug's mother drew her breath in sharply and glanced at his father. "Genetically?" she whispered, then cleared her throat.

Dr. Levison raised a dark eyebrow and looked back and forth from his mother to his father. "Is that a problem?"

For the first time during the two days since the blood tests for his football physical had shown there was something wrong, Mom's eyes filled with tears. She opened her mouth to speak, but no words came out. Finally, she buried her face in her hands.

Dad put an arm around her shoulder and pulled her close. He shook his head slowly, then touched Dr. Levison's shoulder. "May we have a few minutes alone with Doug?"

"Certainly," she said. "I'll be at the nurses' station."

Even though the room was silent after she left, Doug's ears buzzed. Mom and Dad had been so calm about everything. Until now. He took a deep breath of the disinfectant-laden air, then broke the silence. "What's up?" he said, pushing his lips into something he hoped resembled a smile. "First good news I've heard, and you guys—"

Mom's hands dropped to her side, and she lifted her head. Tears streamed down her cheeks, and she clenched her teeth. "We meant to tell you a long time ago, but somehow—" Her voice broke. "We love you so much. It never made any difference, not even after your brothers were born."

Bitter-tasting saliva flooded Doug's mouth. "*What* never made any difference?"

Dad sucked in a deep breath. "We adopted you when you were a week old. We have no idea who your biological parents are."

OFFICIAL RULES TO WINNERS CLASSIC SWEEPSTAKES

No Purchase necessary. To enter the sweepstakes follow instructions found elsewhere in this offer. You can also enter the sweepstakes by hand printing your name, address, city, state and zip code on a 3" x 5" piece of paper and mailing it to: Winners Classic Sweepstakes, P.O. Box 785, Gibbstown, NJ 08027. Mail each entry separately. Sweepstakes begins 12/1/91. Entries must be received by 6/1/93. Some presentations of this sweepstakes may feature a deadline for the Early Bird prize. If the offer you receive does, then to be eligible for the Early Bird prize your entry must be received according to the Early Bird date specified. Not responsible for lost, late, damaged, misdirected, illegible or postage due mail. Mechanically reproduced entries are not eligible. All entries become property of the sponsor and will not be returned.

Prize Selection/Validations: Winners will be selected in random drawings on or about 7/30/93, by VENTURA ASSOCIATES, INC., an independent judging organization whose decisions are final. Odds of winning are determined by total number of entries received. Circulation of this sweepstakes is estimated not to exceed 200 million. Entrants need not be present to win. All prizes are guaranteed to be awarded and delivered to winners. Winners will be notified by mail and may be required to complete an affidavit of eligibility and release of liability which must be returned within 14 days of date of notification or alternate winners will be selected. Any guest of a trip winner will also be required to execute a release of liability. Any prize notification letter or any prize returned to a participating sponsor, Bantam Doubleday Dell Publishing Group, Inc., its participating divisions or subsidiaries, or VENTURA ASSOCIATES, INC. as undeliverable will be awarded to an alternate winner. Prizes are not transferable. No multiple prize winners except as may be necessary due to unavailability, in which case a prize of equal or greater value will be awarded. Prizes will be awarded approximately 90 days after the drawing. All taxes, automobile license and registration fees, if applicable, are the sole responsibility of the winners. Entry constitutes permission (except where prohibited) to use winners' names and likenesses for publicity purposes without further or other compensation.

Participation: This sweepstakes is open to residents of the United States and Canada, except for the province of Quebec. This sweepstakes is sponsored by Bantam Doubleday Dell Publishing Group, Inc. (BDD), 666 Fifth Avenue, New York, NY 10103. Versions of this sweepstakes with different graphics will be offered in conjunction with various solicitations or promotions by different subsidiaries and divisions of BDD. Employees and their families of BDD, its division, subsidiaries, advertising agencies, and VENTURA ASSOCIATES, INC., are not eligible.

Canadian residents, in order to win, must first correctly answer a time limited arithmetical skill testing question. Void in Quebec and wherever prohibited or restricted by law. Subject to all federal, state, local and provincial laws and regulations.

Prizes: The following values for prizes are determined by the manufacturers' suggested retail prices or by what these items are currently known to be selling for at the time this offer was published. Approximate retail values include handling and delivery of prizes. Estimated maximum retail value of prizes: 1 Grand Prize ($27,500 if merchandise or $25,000 Cash); 1 First Prize ($3,000); 5 Second Prizes ($400 each); 35 Third Prizes ($100 each); 1,000 Fourth Prizes ($9.00 each); 1 Early Bird Prize ($5,000); Total approximate maximum retail value is $50,000. Winners will have the option of selecting any prize offered at level won. Automobile winner must have a valid driver's license at the time the car is awarded. Trips are subject to space and departure availability. Certain black-out dates may apply. Travel must be completed within one year from the time the prize is awarded. Minors must be accompanied by an adult. Prizes won by minors will be awarded in the name of parent or legal guardian.

For a list of Major Prize Winners (available after 7/30/93): send a self-addressed, stamped envelope entirely separate from your entry to: Winners Classic Sweepstakes Winners, P.O. Box 825, Gibbstown, NJ 08027. Requests must be received by 6/1/93. DO NOT SEND ANY OTHER CORRESPONDENCE TO THIS P.O. BOX.

Women's Fiction

On Sale in March

ONCE AN ANGEL

☐ 29409-1 $5.50/6.50 in Canada

by Teresa Medeiros

Bestselling author of HEATHER AND VELVET

A captivating historical romance that sweeps from the wilds of an exotic paradise to the elegance of Victorian England. "Teresa Medeiros writes rare love stories to cherish."
— *Romantic Times*

IN A ROGUE'S ARMS

☐ 29692-2 $4.99/5.99 in Canada

by Virginia Brown writing as Virginia Lynn
Author of LYON'S PRIZE

A passion-filled retelling of the beloved Robin Hood tale, set in Texas of the 1870's. The first of Bantam's new "Once Upon a Time" romances: passionate historical romances with themes from fairy tales, myths, and legends.

THE LADY AND THE CHAMP

☐ 29655-8 $4.99/5.99 in Canada

by Fran Baker

Bestselling Loveswept author Fran Baker's first mainstream romance! The passionate story of a boxer/lawyer and the interior decorator who inherited his gym — and won his heart. "Unforgettable...a warm, wonderful knockout of a book."
— *Julie Garwood*